# Fifth Grade:
## Here Comes Trouble

# Fifth Grade: Here Comes Trouble

## Colleen O'Shaughnessy McKenna

AN
**APPLE**
PAPERBACK

SCHOLASTIC INC.
New York Toronto London Auckland Sydney

0-590-41734-7

12 11 10 9 8                                    4 5 6/9

This book is dedicated with all my best wishes and heartfelt gratitude to Marilyn Hollinshead and her Writing Workshop at Pinocchio Bookstore, and to my weekly writers' group, Unclaimed Treasures, for supplying me with hefty doses of criticism and love.

# Chapter One

"But why would you even *want* to invite boys to your birthday party?" Collette flopped back against the small mountain of white pillows on Marsha's bed. "You said we were going to Skateland to celebrate."

"We still are," laughed Marsha. "Only now, five of the cutest boys in the whole fifth grade will be with us! Just think of it, Collette . . . my party is only a week away . . . seven little days." Marsha hugged herself and laughed again. "I can hardly wait!"

Collette nodded her head gloomily. Only seven days. . . .

"Marsha, a person is supposed to invite *friends* to a birthday party. . . ."

"Boys *are* friends."

"How can you be friends with someone who eats chalk?"

Collette picked up a ruffled pillow and punched it gently with her fist. Having boys at Marsha's party was going to ruin everything. How could she have a fun time skating when she had to worry about a bunch of rude boys trying to trip her? And there was no *way* she would stand and do the Hokey Pokey, while a bunch of boys just waited for the girls to put their rear ends in and shake them all about.

Marsha stood up and began swaying dreamily around the room.

"Can you picture John holding my hand tightly as we skate to romantic music? This will be a party that will go down in the history of my family."

"Gross," muttered Collette, turning her head away. She had known Marsha since nursery school, and now, just because she was going to be eleven years old, Marsha was acting like a complete stranger!

"It's finally here, Collette," sighed Marsha. "At last . . . the year of my signpost has arrived!"

"Signpost?"

Collette slipped off the bed and walked slowly around the room. Where in the world was Marsha going to put a *signpost*? Just about everything you could buy was already crammed into Marsha's bedroom — stereo, VCR, even a fancy gold phone like the ones rich ladies used in the movies.

Marsha piled her long dark hair on top of her head and looked up at Collette. "What do you think, Collette? Should I get my hair cut before the party or just wear it up? I don't want to look too childish for my signpost."

"I don't think a signpost really cares how you look, Marsha," snapped Collette, grabbing her jacket from the bed. "Why do you keep talking about this signpost business, anyway?"

"What . . . what?" sputtered Marsha. She hopped off the window seat, planting both hands on her hips. "Weren't you listening to one word I said this morning? I explained the whole thing to you on the phone, Collette."

"Oh yeah, that's right. Something about your great, great grandmother starting some birthday gimmick. . . ."

"Holy moly!" shouted Marsha. She shook her

finger at Collette. "Don't you dare call my family's signpost a . . . a gimmick. You should have felt privileged I even told you about it. It's sacred, private, and very history-filled!"

"Well . . . sorry, Marsha." Collette tried to look more interested. "I really was trying to listen to you on the phone, but my brother Stevie kept pulling the receiver away from my ear. He was trying to see your face through the wires."

"Phooey," snorted Marsha as she bounced down on her bed. "I poured out a century of family tradition to a measly four-year-old. Don't ever let Stevie near that phone when I'm on it again, Collette! For Pete's sake, can't your mom control those kids over there?"

Collette frowned. It made her mad when Marsha threw darts at her family. Since Marsha was an only child, she thought the Murphy's house, with its four children, was a noisy, wild zoo!

"So tell me again about the signpost." Collette sat down on the edge of the bed and nodded her head like she was ready for all the facts.

Actually, she was. The signpost business was probably why Marsha was suddenly interested in boys. Maybe once all the facts were laid out, Col-

4

lette could figure out a way to convince Marsha not to invite a single boy to her party.

Collette smiled, almost laughing. She was feeling better already. She wasn't trying to be mean. Boys were okay, especially if you kept them at school, where they belonged. But bringing them to a private birthday party would be just awful. The whole party would be so fakey. Everyone would be trying to act like teenagers in a TV video.

"So tell me," Collette urged.

Marsha sighed. She still looked a little grumpy. Marsha was used to her parents hanging on her every word. "Well, this is the *last* time I'm going to tell you, so be sure to pay attention. And don't tell your little sister or Jeff and Stevie. They would make plans to sabotage my party, I just know it."

Collette stifled a low growl. Her brothers might be a pain in the neck to Collette, but that was because they were little brothers and thought it was fun to bother her. But they certainly wouldn't make trouble for the neighbors. They weren't criminals!

"In our family, the Cessanos . . ." began Marsha. She cleared her throat a couple of times and then started talking in a loud clear voice like she was giving a science report, ". . . there is a very special, wonderful tradition. When a child turns eleven years old, he or she is given a Signpost to Maturity party. It's a very important occasion, which shows the whole world that childhood is almost over and" — Marsha nudged Collette in the side with her elbow — "that when you turn the corner by the signpost, you will be all grown up."

Marsha sat up straighter, folded her hands on her lap, and waited as if she expected applause.

"Get it? Being grown up is around the corner; signposts are usually on corners . . . get it, Collette?"

"That's nice," said Collette politely. She still didn't "get it," really. Where did having boys at the birthday party fit in?

"So, that's why this birthday party has to be so different. It can't be exactly like my others, even though I have always had really great, great parties."

"But why are you having boys?" Collette blurted out.

"The boys *are* the signpost, you dummy!" exploded Marsha. It was easy to see Marsha was getting mad. She always shoved her bangs up with her fist when she was ready to flip on the rage button.

"Boy, oh boy, oh boy!" grumbled Marsha, beginning to pace. "I knew I was making a big mistake by telling you about my party. I should have told Sarah first. She is grown-up enough to realize what a wonderful idea it is!"

Collette twisted the ring on her little finger. She was grown-up, just as grown-up as Sarah. They were best friends.

Besides, inviting a bunch of wild, noisy boys who would just want to throw icing in girls' hair didn't have a thing to do with being grown-up.

"I bet you'd be thrilled if I changed my plans and rented Boo-Boo the clown to come over here and blow up balloons for my guests, wouldn't you?" Marsha turned to see how that registered with Collette. "Or maybe I could bring in Checkers the pony. Wouldn't that be a great signpost?"

Collette stood up and put her hand on the door. "Oh, go ask a million, trillion boys to your party, Marsha. I don't care. I think it's a dumb idea, that's all."

Marsha gave a smug smile and shook her head. She was acting like a smart teacher with all the answers, talking to poor dumb Collette Murphy, who just couldn't seem to get a few simple facts through her head.

"You just don't understand the seriousness of the signpost party, Collette. My mom had a migraine headache for three straight days when she found out I couldn't use her signpost. Try thinking about my poor mom, Collette. Think how she must feel. She saved her signpost for me all these years, and now I can't use it." Marsha's voice trailed off sadly.

"Oh, use it anyway," suggested Collette, beginning to brighten. If Marsha used Mrs. Cessano's signpost, whatever it was, then the boys wouldn't be needed after all! Everything could go back to normal.

Marsha slumped into a rosebud-print chair, her head in her hand. She looked awful, like she was about to get sick.

"I can't, Collette." Marsha looked up. There was something tragic about her face all of a sudden. "My mother's signpost was her first bra! A lovely little white-lace bra with a perfect pink rose attached to the center."

"A . . . bra?"

Marsha nodded. "She still has it wrapped in yellow cellophane in the bottom of her sock drawer."

"A bra!" repeated Collette, almost joyously. "A bra would be perfect, Marsha! I like it. Yeah, a bra is symbolic, traditional. . . ."

Collette stopped. She was going to add "and completely private." At last, a signpost that wouldn't have to involve the whole fifth grade!

"I can't," sighed Marsha, sitting up straighter and shaking her head. "I'm still as flat as your two brothers."

Collette hated to admit it, but Marsha was right.

"My mom said I may take after my Aunt Edna. She's almost fifty and she still doesn't need a bra."

"Hey, what about braces?" suggested Collette. "Lots of seventh- and eighth-graders have braces. They are really grown-up looking."

Marsha opened her mouth to flash two rows of perfectly straight, white teeth.

"Good teeth run in my family, Collette. On both sides."

Marsha reached over and grabbed a thick tablet from the dresser. "Come on. We have to start planning my party."

"Oh yeah, the party," muttered Collette. She didn't even *try* to hide the groan in her voice.

"There you go again," growled Marsha, pointing a ballpoint pen directly into Collette's face. "My cousin Carole predicted this would happen. Carole said you're scared to death of any boy who isn't your brother!"

Heat rose so quickly up Collette's neck, it almost shot out her forehead.

"What does Carole know?"

"Plenty. Carole is thirteen years old, which makes her a legal teenager! Carole has been to my house lots and lots of times, Collette, so she has practically seen you grow up."

Collette crossed her arms and made a face at Marsha. Carole did not know her. Not at all. Every time Carole came to Marsha's house she just sat on the wicker swing and made fun of all the Murphys from across the street. Carole thought she was so special and smart, just because she happened to be born a couple of years ahead of Collette.

"Carole said last night that you would hate my party because you were an old fuddy-duddy."

"I am not!"

Marsha nodded, pleased with the way things were going. "And Carole said that it's a real shame you're a fuddy-duddy 'cause with your long blonde hair, you're kind of pretty."

"She did?" Carole never said anything like that to Collette's face. She was always making cracks about the generic clothes Collette wore and how it was so sad that Collette was practically a non-paid baby-sitter at the Murphy house.

"Carole thinks you have real . . . real potential, but you just don't know what to do with it."

Collette zippered her jacket. "Well, tell Carole she wears too much makeup, and if that's called potential, then I don't want it."

Marsha crossed her arms and stared up at the ceiling, tapping her tennis shoe and looking smug again.

"Hah! Even if you *wanted* to wear makeup, you wouldn't be allowed to, Collette. Your mom won't even let you wear lip gloss and you know it. You are stuck living in that zoo with two crazy brothers and you have to share a room with a puny six-year-old sister. Face it, Collette, you do not have a normal life."

Collette scowled as she flung open the bedroom

door. Boy, was she glad she lived right across the street so she wasn't trapped here another second.

"Wait a minute, Collette! Where are you going?" wailed Marsha. "You have to stay and help me call the boys to invite them."

Collette shuddered. Calling boys was probably the last thing in the world she wanted to do. She would rather eat raw liver for breakfast, or help her mom clean Stevie's stinky tennis shoes.

You couldn't just plug your nose when you called boys.

"I have to go home."

Marsha waved Collette away. "Oh, go ahead. Run on home to Mommy," she continued in a singsong voice. "Carole bet me five bucks that you wouldn't call a single boy. She said you wouldn't even show up at my birthday party. That's how smart she is."

The knuckles on Collette's hand went white as she squeezed the banister with all her might.

"And listen to this, Collette. My very own mother said that she was glad . . . downright thankful, that I don't make straight A's like you. She thinks your brain is too developed for the rest of you. And now it's messing you up. That's why you hate the idea of a boy-girl party so much."

Collette looked over her shoulder and frowned as hard as she could. Marsha's mother shouldn't be talking about her. Besides, her brain and the rest of her were working just fine together.

"A true, normal, all-American fifth-grader would be excited about this party," continued Marsha. She stood as close as she could to Collette on the stairs. "The whole thing is based on hormones . . . scads and scads of hormones. And since you are the youngest one in the whole class, you don't have as many as the rest of us."

Marsha paused. Collette hated the way Marsha always waited for her insults to sink in.

"You just don't have as many hormones as Sarah and me," declared Marsha proudly.

"It's Sarah and *I*," snapped Collette. "And since Sarah is my very best friend, we have the exact same amount of everything!"

Why did Marsha have to be so mean all the time? If she didn't live right across the street, Collette would never want to see her again.

Collette stomped down the steps and out the

front door. She was so mad she pounded every step of the way across the street and up her driveway.

Marsha thought she knew everything!

As Collette yanked open the side door, she threw one final scowl across the street at Marsha's house.

Marsha's signpost party wasn't going to mess up *her* life. Collette would make sure of that!

# Chapter Two

As soon as Collette got on the bus Monday morning, she could tell Marsha was still clinging to her bad mood like a favorite toy. Marsha sighed loudly and then sighed again as she slid across the seat to make room for Collette.

"Boy, am I tired, Collette. I was up till ten o'clock making my phone calls. Then I had to make a list of things to say when everyone else runs out of stuff to talk about at the party."

Marsha slapped her book bag and shoved her face into Collette's. "This party is so much work. Too bad you had your old temper tantrum and stormed off. I could have used your help."

Collette shrugged, refusing to feel the least bit guilty.

"Sorry, Marsha. Next time, just call your cousin Carole."

"I did, but she had to baby-sit her little brother."

Collette smiled. Knowing Carole had a younger brother somewhere made her seem a little bit more human.

"Well. . . ."

"Well, what?" asked Collette.

"Well, don't you want to hear all about me calling the boys?" Marsha giggled and squirmed closer to Collette. She lowered her voice. "I called James first. Boy oh boy, was he excited. I didn't want to invite him cause his fingernails are always so dirty, but my mom plays bridge with his mom so. . . . Then I called Roger. He was his usual rude self, but I had to invite him because the other boys think he's so funny. I waited to call John McKechnie last!"

Collette studied her shoes, not wanting Marsha to see that she was a teeny bit interested in what John had to say about the party. John was sort of the king of the fifth grade. The boys liked him because he was a good athlete. The girls liked him because he was the most handsome boy in the world.

And if John wasn't going to the party, no one would want to go.

"Are you listening to me?" Marsha jabbed her elbow into Collette's side.

"What?"

Marsha groaned so loudly, a seventh-grader turned around to glare at her.

"I said that John asked if he could bring Susannah. She's a seventh-grader! I nearly choked!"

Collette grinned. She had seen John and Susannah standing together in the cafeteria. Susannah was at least four inches taller than John.

"So what did you say to him when he asked?"

Marsha snorted. "I told him that he couldn't, of course. After all, my mother is footing the bill for this great party. It will probably cost five or six hundred dollars. I think I should be able to call all the shots!"

The school bus slowed and turned onto Walnut Street. From the window, Collette could see Sarah standing with a group of girls outside the school.

"Oh good, there's Sarah!" announced Marsha. She pounded on the window with her fist. "I can hardly wait to tell her about my party. I tried to get her last night but she was out and then I had all those boys to call. . . ."

As soon as the bus stopped, Collette grabbed her book bag and pushed herself into the aisle. Luckily Marsha was too busy pounding and yelling through the window to notice, because Collette wanted to get to Sarah first. She needed a few minutes alone with Sarah to warn her about the boy-girl party. Sarah would be just as upset as Collette. Sarah knew that boys could really mess things up, just by being boys.

"Collette! Collette, over here!" cried Sarah. She was hopping up and down behind Eric Nelson, who was one of the tallest kids in the whole school.

"I've been waiting for you," laughed Sarah. She reached out and pulled Collette next to her.

Instantly the knot in Collette's stomach began to loosen. Good old Sarah. Collette felt better already, just standing next to her, knowing that they were both exactly the same inside.

"I have got to talk to you," whispered Collette. She giggled nervously. Wait until Sarah heard about the party! She would howl and then make a funny crack about Marsha trying to act so grown-up.

18

Collette looked over her shoulder, trying to spot Marsha. She didn't want her sneaking up on them.

Marsha was already in the middle of a group of fifth-graders, waving her arms around and nodding her head this way and that. She was probably bragging about how she had handled John and the seventh-grader.

"We have to do something about Marsha," began Collette. "She has a horrible plan all dreamed up to invite boys to her birthday party and — "

"I know!"

Collette's smile shot away like a rubber band. Sarah knew?

"Marsha called Kiersten, and Kiersten called Meg, and when I saw Danielle at the mall she told me all about it! I can't believe it. I can't believe Marsha is so brave to . . . to call boys and ask them to come over to her house."

Marsha, brave? Brave? That certainly wasn't the word Collette had hoped Sarah would use at a time like this.

*Dumb* was what Collette had hoped for.

"Is Marsha going to have us play a game or two at her house before the skating party?" asked

Sarah eagerly. "Just so it isn't spin-the-bottle!"

Collette's book bag slid down to her fingertips. Suddenly she was so weak she could hardly hold it.

Here was Sarah, her best friend, Sarah, actually excited about Marsha's birthday party. Sarah could hardly wait to hear every little fact about the boys!

"John McKechnie will never come to a fifth-grade party," said Sarah solemnly. "I heard he goes to seventh-grade parties with Susannah Thacker!"

Collette followed Sarah's eyes, and they both stared at John, standing in the middle of a bunch of fifth- and sixth-grade boys.

Collette nodded. John was probably too cute for the fifth grade.

"Well, if he's smart, he sure won't go to Marsha's party," said Collette flatly. "It's going to be so dumb, Sarah."

"Not really."

Collette let her book bag drop to the pavement. "I can't believe you are getting this excited about it."

Sarah smiled weakly. "It could be a lot of fun, Collette."

Collette shuddered and picked up her book bag. She was beginning to feel very alone all of a sudden.

"Sarah! Sarah!" shouted Marsha. She broke in between the two girls and hugged Sarah, swinging her around.

"I bet you two are talking about my great party, right?"

"Right," mumbled Collette. Was there anything else in the whole world to talk about *but* the great party?

"Oh, Marsha, everyone is so excited!" squealed Sarah. Both girls hopped up and down, gripping each other's arms as if they had just won the lottery. "Amanda called me last night when I got back from the mall, and Lorraine called me this morning before school!"

Collette's heart sank an inch. Nobody had bothered to call *her* last night. Not even Sarah.

Marsha had probably alerted every girl in the class that Collette was the official party pooper.

She took a step back. It sounded like the entire

fifth grade was delirious with happiness about boys coming to the party. Everyone but Collette Murphy.

"I knew you would be happy, Sarah," said Marsha. She turned and jerked a thumb toward Collette. "I guess you can tell that Collette is not the least bit excited about my party. I'm going to all this work, just to have the most wonderful boy-girl party in the city and Collette is . . . is actually *mad* at me for it."

"I'm not mad," pointed out Collette. "I just think it's not a good idea."

"Not a good idea," repeated Marsha, wagging her head from side to side. "Your idea of a good time is going to Chuckie Cheese with your brothers and sister. Whooptie-do!"

Collette watched Sarah, hoping she would get mad at Marsha for insulting her, but Sarah was twirling her hair and grinning like it was Christmas morning.

"So, which boys did you pick?" asked Sarah. She was acting like Collette wasn't even there.

"Petey, Roger," Marsha made a face. "I had to ask Roger, but my mom promised to yell at him if he gets too rude. Let me see, David, Patrick, and . . ." Marsha closed her eyes like she was praying, "and John McKechnie!"

Sarah nodded. Collette could tell by the way Sarah was smiling that she approved of the list.

"Now listen to this, girls," ordered Marsha. She reached out and drew both girls back into a huddle. "I want to get one thing straight. I get to be the first one to skate with John, since I'm the birthday girl."

"Sure, sure," agreed Sarah readily. "In fact . . . since this is my first boy-girl party, I may just watch."

A sudden surge of happiness flooded through Collette. She smiled at Sarah. She wanted to toss her book bag high into the air and hug her. Good old Sarah! She did feel exactly the same way as Collette about the boys coming. Sarah was just trying to be polite for Marsha's sake, that's all.

Collette stood up a little straighter and grinned. She and Sarah could both go to the party and watch together. It wouldn't be so awkward if the two of them stuck together.

"Sarah Messland, you dirty double-crosser!" exploded Marsha. "Friday night you promised me on the phone that if I asked boys to my party, you would ask Petey to skate!"

Sarah's face colored. Collette's stomach fell. Petey? Sarah would ask Petey Bennett to skate?

"I didn't promise, Marsha," protested Sarah. "I said that *maybe* I would ask him if everyone else asked a boy. . . ."

"You said Petey had the cutest dimples in the world and that he wasn't half as gross as Roger or James," reminded Marsha. Marsha stared straight at Collette while she said it.

Collette looked at Sarah. Sarah thought a boy was cute and hadn't even bothered to tell Collette first?

Collette felt wounded inside. A best friend rule had just been broken.

Sarah must have known that telling the "Petey" news to someone like Marsha would be more fun. Marsha would be a better audience.

"Boy, I'll look like a real geek if I'm the only one skating with a boy," wailed Marsha. "It will look like — like my wedding reception or something."

Sarah laughed.

"It isn't funny, Sarah," snapped Marsha. "I knew this would happen! Collette has already talked you out of liking my party. Thanks to you two, my signpost party will turn out to be a big, fat fizzle!"

Marsha hugged her book bag to her chest. "Wait until my cousin Carole hears about this! She tried to warn me about my baby friends."

"I'm not a baby!" Sarah said softly. She drew her eyebrows together and looked a little worried.

"Maybe I can ask Carole to bring some of her teenage friends to my party so John McKechnie won't think he's in the middle of a nursery school field trip."

"Maybe I'll ask Petey to skate one time if Collette asks a boy, too." Sarah looked over at Collette and smiled hopefully.

"Hah!" spat out Marsha in a mean voice. "Sarah, if you wait for Collette Murphy to ask a boy to skate, you'll die an old maid. Collette is *afraid* of boys, in case you haven't noticed!"

Marsha raised her eyebrows and shot both girls a final scowl before she turned and marched off toward the school.

"Wow, does that woman have a temper!"

shouted Roger. He bumped into both girls with his elbows, knocking their book bags to the ground.

"Watch out, Roger!" warned Sarah. She rubbed her elbow and bent to pick up her book bag. "Gross, look at all this stuff on the bottom of my bag!"

"Just a little mud." Roger reached out and slapped Sarah on the back. "Be tough, be strong!"

"Hey, that hurts!" Sarah moved away and shook her head at Roger.

"Sorry!" cried Roger holding up both hands like he was about to be arrested. "I had no idea you were so breakable!"

Collette giggled at the fake concern in Roger's voice. Roger was rude all right, but he was kind of funny, too.

"Why don't you go stand in the middle of Penn Avenue and play tag with a bus," snapped Sarah, brushing off her sweater.

Roger grinned and wagged a finger back at her. "You'd better watch it, Sarah. You are beginning to sound just like Marsha."

Collette felt a chill run down her back. Roger was just saying that to be mean. Sarah wasn't like

Marsha at all. Sarah and Collette were best friends; they were exactly alike.

"You'd better be nice to me or I won't skate with you at the big party on Saturday," continued Roger.

"Don't you dare get *near* me at the party," said Sarah.

"Fine with me," insisted Roger, backing away. "I'll have to save all of my skates for . . . for Collette, here. She's the only one left in the fifth grade with manners."

Roger turned and ran across the playground, hopping onto John McKechnie's back and waving an imaginary lasso.

"Roger should be locked up in the Highland Park Zoo," declared Sarah. Sarah watched John pull Roger off. Both boys were laughing.

Collette watched, too, a small frown beginning to grow. Boys seemed to have so much fun all the time. They didn't worry about half the stuff girls did. It didn't really seem fair.

"Why don't you ask John to skate at the party?" suggested Sarah. "He's so nice."

Collette's head shot up. Ask John McKechnie to skate?

"John thinks you're the smartest girl in the whole class, Collette. He told me last year. He said he likes correcting your papers 'cause he never has to waste any ink marking things wrong."

Oh, wonderful, thought Collette. So he would certainly rather skate with Collette Murphy than Susannah Thacker, who has thick black hair hanging all the way down her back.

Sarah didn't even seen to notice when Collette didn't answer. She was staring at the boys tossing a Nerf football over by the parking lot. Sarah almost clapped when Petey caught a pass.

Sarah *did* like Petey. She must like him a lot to want to skate with him and watch him play football on the playground.

"So, when did you realize you like Petey Bennett?" asked Collette. Her own voice surprised her. It sounded cool and sophisticated and very mean. Just like the voices of ladies on the soap operas when they asked, "So, when did you start dating my husband?"

Sarah turned away from the football game and stared at Collette. She opened both eyes a little wider and studied Collette as if she had just said a swear word.

"I can't believe you told Marsha you liked Petey and you never even told me you thought he was nice."

Sarah shrugged. "I told you this summer that I saw him at my swimming pool with James."

Collette shook her head. "You said he was wearing sick-looking swim trunks and that he threw an Italian ice at you. That is all you said, Sarah."

Sarah nodded her head. "I know. *That* was telling you I liked him. . . kinda."

"What?" Collette couldn't tell if she was getting mad or about to laugh. "Since when does throwing food at someone mean you like them?"

"He doesn't like me, but I like him . . . kind of. Oh, forget it."

Collette blew out a deep breath. "Oh, well, excuse me if I am having a hard time understanding all the technical rules about what a person does and does not do when he likes another person." Collette waited a second, then took another deep breath and went on. "And since I am so dumb in the boy department, I guess I should just expect for you to call Marsha the next time anything romantic happens, like Petey throwing a baloney sandwich at you."

Sarah laughed.

"It isn't funny, Sarah." Collette tried to keep her voice as mad as possible, so Sarah couldn't tell how close she was to crying.

None of this was funny. None of it.

Sarah shifted her book bag from one hand to the other. She raked her long reddish hair back with her fingers. Finally she shrugged.

"I wasn't trying to be sneaky or anything like that, Collette. I didn't think you would be interested in hearing about Petey, that's all." Sarah scratched her head. She was looking everywhere but at Collette. "You and I never talk about boys and stuff like that."

Of course not, Collette thought. Why would you bother telling me when you know how immature I am? I couldn't *possibly* understand a thing about a boy-girl relationship.

"Petey gave me an eraser he found in a cereal box this morning," offered Sarah. She giggled and tried to smile right into Collette's face as if this news flash would make up for all the news flashes that Collette had missed out on in the past.

It didn't.

"Who cares?" cried Collette hotly. She swung

her book bag across her shoulder. As she turned away, the book bag bumped into Sarah's arm.

Collette didn't even stop to say, "Sorry."

She wasn't sorry for anything except that Marsha had to have a signpost party in the first place. It was all Marsha's fault.

This party was a signpost all right. A signpost to trouble!

# Chapter Three

By Wednesday it was a well-known fact that ten of the girls and five of the cutest boys in the fifth grade were coming to Marsha's signpost birthday party. They were to report to Marsha's house at three for cake and presents, and then Mrs. Cessano and Marsha's aunt would drive them to Skateland for three hours of skating.

By Wednesday everybody also knew not to mention the party to Collette Murphy. It was as though Marsha had sent out a memo to everyone explaining that Collette was a party pooper but she had to be invited because she lived right across the street.

In a way Collette was glad. It made it easier to

pretend that Saturday would never arrive. But Sarah was going right along with the others in not talking about the party, which wasn't so nice. Sarah still saved Collette a seat at lunch and smiled at her whenever their eyes met during class, but it wasn't the same. Collette watched as Sarah and Amanda threw an apple core inside Petey's locker, and saw how Marsha and Sarah would look at each other and laugh whenever John McKechnie stopped and asked them for directions to Marsha's house, or what he should wear.

No one bothered to run up to Collette and giggle about what they were wearing to the party, or call her right after school to ask who she might ask to skate with during the couples' skate.

The week dragged by, and by Friday Collette came home from school convinced she had a fever.

"Feel my head, Mom," Collette suggested. "I'm burning up. I told the nurse, but she said I was okay."

Mother set the laundry basket down on the bottom step and reached out her hand.

"You're fine, Collette. Go get some juice and sit on the couch for a while. You're probably just excited about the party."

"Excited?" Collette tried to give a short laugh to let her mother know exactly how wrong she was. "I don't even want to go to the party," said Collette slowly.

Mother smiled, giving Collette's shoulder a little squeeze.

"That's just because Marsha is making such a big deal about the boys coming. You know Marsha, she wants to make everything a big production."

It surprised Collette that her mom knew about the boys. Collette had deliberately not told her it was a boy-girl party.

"Mrs. Cessano called me today and talked for nearly an hour. She went out and bought a new video camera, just to film the group." Mrs. Murphy laughed and shook her head.

Collette smiled. Her mom probably thought the whole idea was dumb, too. In fact, she probably thought it was so dumb that she wouldn't care a bit if Collette just stayed home on Saturday.

"Marsha said her mom ordered a three-tier

birthday cake with a plastic girl on top standing next to a traffic light," added Collette.

Mrs. Murphy looked puzzled.

"The bakery didn't have any signposts, so Mrs. Cessano just put a traffic light on top of the cake . . . to stand for the signpost."

Mrs. Murphy thought for a second, then smiled and nodded her head as if she thought Mrs. Cessano had been clever.

"The whole idea of a signpost party sure is corny, isn't it, Mom?" Collette was so glad to finally have someone to talk to about the dumbness of Marsha's party. Everyone at school would have thought she was some sort of traitor if she said one word against it.

But her mom would agree with Collette. In fact, she had probably felt the same way when she was ten years old.

"Isn't it dumb, Mom?" asked Collette. "To invite boys, to pretend Marsha is all grown-up — just because she's turning eleven?"

"Well, not really," began her mother. She picked up the laundry basket and thought for a minute. "You've known the boys in your class for almost six years; they are your friends, and. . . ."

"No, they aren't!" Collette could hardly get the words out fast enough. "It's like we're two different tribes in the jungle, Mom. . . ."

Mrs. Murphy started to laugh out loud. The real loud, throw-your-head-back, ha-ha-ha kind of laugh.

"What's funny?" asked Jeff. He practically ran down the hall from the kitchen.

"Tell me, Mommy," asked Laura. She laughed without even knowing what was funny.

"Nothing is funny," snapped Collette. She was not about to discuss this party with her brothers and little sister.

"Oh, Collette," Mother laughed again and wiped her eyes. "You're funny — "

"I want to know the joke," demanded Stevie. He pushed Collette back and hung onto Mother's leg. "Tell me."

"Collette and I were just talking — "

"It's none of your business, Stevie!" announced Collette. "Don't tell them, Mom. I was trying to talk to you in *private!*"

Jeff poked Collette on the right shoulder. "Well, no secrets, right Mom?"

36

Stevie spun around and waved his small fist at Collette.

Mother started up the stairs. "Go back and finish your snack, kids. Collette, come on up and we'll finish talking."

Laura slid onto the bottom step. "No fair. I want to hear the secret, too."

"It's not a secret," said Mother quickly. "Go finish your juice, Laura. Collette and Mommy just want to talk about Marsha's party, that's all."

"Oh, I get it." Jeff laughed and rubbed his hands together like a witch over a pot of bubbling stew. "Yeah, Collette is worried 'cause everyone at school thinks she's a scaredy-cat."

Collette spun around so quickly she fell into Stevie.

"Get off me, scaredy-cat." Stevie started to laugh at his own joke.

"Don't tease, Jeff," Mother called back over her shoulder.

Jeff poked Collette again, jumping back and pointing at her. "Ha-ha-ha-ha. . . . Keto and I heard Sarah and Marsha talking about you on the playground this morning."

"You did?" Collette felt a sudden stab of fear.

"Yeah, Marsha said you would be the only girl not skating with a boy at her party. She said you were a scaredy-cat."

"Collette is not a scaredy-cat!" shouted Laura from the bottom step.

"What did Sarah say back?" asked Collette. If Sarah agreed with Marsha then she wouldn't be Collette's best friend anymore, ever. Let her be best friends with Marsha for the rest of her life.

"Sarah just told Marsha to leave you alone."

"She did?" Collette reached out and grabbed Jeff's arm. "Did she get mad at Marsha and tell her to be quiet and leave me alone and stop talking about the party — ?"

"Let go, Collette!" Jeff pulled his arm free and backed away. "Sarah just said to leave you alone, that's all. Stop making such a big deal out of it."

"Well, it is a *big deal*, Jeff Murphy!" shouted Collette. "None of you know how much of a big deal it is 'cause you're . . . little babies and you don't know anything about how stupid the fifth grade can be."

Collette stopped, waiting for her voice to stop shaking.

"Collette, calm down," ordered Mother from the landing. "I am getting a little tired of hearing about Marsha's party. Jeff is right, stop making such a big deal about it. Go to the party, have fun, come home. . . . It's not the end of the world."

"But, it is!" cried Collette. She saw Laura jump back on the seat, her eyes growing larger by the second. Stevie covered both ears with his hands and raced back into the kitchen.

"I am losing my best friend, the girls in my class won't talk about things in front of me, and my very own family is laughing at me." Collette was glad huge tears were streaming down her face. Maybe now her family would realize what a truly *big deal* this whole boy-girl party was!

Laura buried her face in her hands and started to cry, while Mother hurried down the rest of the stairs.

"Honey, relax, you are upsetting yourself over nothing."

"Nothing," sobbed Collette. "You don't have to go to the awful party."

As Mother reached out to hug Collette, Jeff took a step closer. "Sarah still likes you, Collette," he offered, reaching over and giving her an awkward pat on the arm. "Even if the rest of the girls don't."

"Oh, *thank* you, Jeff," sobbed Collette loudly. "Thanks for nothing!"

"Jeff didn't mean it the way it sounded, Collette," said Mother quickly.

A sudden crash from the kitchen broke up the hug. Collette looked down the hall to see Stevie standing, holding a large piece of a coffee mug. "Sorry, Mommy. I was only trying to get Collette some juice," he cried. Orange juice soaked dark blue blotches into his jeans. "It wasn't my fault."

"Oh, Stevie . . ." Mother sighed as she hurried down the hall. "Don't touch anything till I clean up the glass. Oh great — the phone's ringing . . . Stevie, don't move." Collette glanced from Jeff to Laura. Both of them were watching her to see if she was going to crack up again.

"Marsha's party sounds dumb," said Jeff quietly.

Collette tried to smile.

"Real dumb!" added Laura. She smiled up at Collette. "I hate her party!"

"Telephone for you, Collette!" called Mother from the kitchen.

Mother held the phone out, a sympathetic smile on her face. Collette was able to smile back. In fact, she felt much better now that she had admitted the awfulness of Marsha's party to her family.

Her mother knew now that the party wasn't going to be any fun for Collette and she would probably insist that Collette just stay home. The whole family could rent a movie and sit around and eat big bowls of popcorn and have a great time.

"Thanks, Mom!" Collette said cheerfully, glad a plan had finally fallen into place.

"It's Marsha," whispered Mother, pushing the phone into Collette's hand. "Now *try* to act more excited about her party, honey."

The phone nearly fell from Collette's hand. Her mother wanted her to fake excitement about the stupid party. Did that mean her mother was a little ashamed that her daughter was the only one in the fifth grade who wasn't truly thrilled to pieces over Marsha's party?

"Hello . . ." Collette deliberately tried to make her voice sound as unexcited as she could.

Mother's quick sigh stuck in her throat and escaped as a hiss. She shook her head and gave Collette a disappointed look.

Collette turned away, facing the wall. Suddenly she felt completely deserted. First the fifth grade, then the world, and now even her mom were against her.

A small, sad tremor moved through Collette.

Why were there signposts in the world anyway? All they did was remind people that some of them were falling behind the rest of the crowd. Marsha and her mean cousin Carole were probably right after all. Collette wasn't a bit ready for a boy-girl party and not one bit of her wanted to *get* ready.

Tomorrow afternoon Skateland rink would be filled with fifth-graders, boys and girls, holding on to each other's hands and liking it. Everyone would laugh and point at Collette Murphy as they whizzed past. Collette Murphy, standing in the corner like a scaredy-cat.

"Collette? Collette?" shouted Marsha at the other end of the phone. "Are you listening?"

"Yeah."

"Get over here right away. You'll never guess who is sitting right in the middle of my bedroom, waiting to help us plan my great birthday party."

Collette didn't have to guess. She could hear Carole's laughter across the telephone wires.

Collette closed her eyes as she tried to suck in some strength.

The party was less than twenty-four hours away. Not nearly time enough to try and find a way out of going to the dumbest party in fifth-grade history.

# Chapter Four

"Carole says the first thing we have to do is to go to the mall and get a few teenagey things," Marsha rattled on at the other end of the phone. "You know, nail polish, hair spray, a few teen magazines to lay around. Wait till you see all the cool stuff Carole is loaning me for my room. You won't believe it!"

Collette pulled the phone away from her ear as Carole and Marsha laughed their heads off.

"Let me see Marsha's face!" begged Stevie. He tugged on the phone wires until Collette lowered it.

"Where is your eyeball, Marsha?" he shouted

into the receiver. He pressed his own eye as close as he could to the receiver. "Say something, Marsha. I can't see you!"

"Collette Murphy!" screamed Marsha. Stevie jumped backwards and dropped the phone onto the hardwood floor.

Collette couldn't help but giggle as she yanked up the cord and put the phone back to her ear.

"I'm here, go on."

"I'm sick of that little brother of yours! What a creep!" snapped Marsha.

If Carole hadn't been sitting in Marsha's bedroom, Marsha would never have said anything that mean about Stevie. Even though Stevie got in lots of trouble, he was so cute with his curly blond hair and pale blue eyes, nobody could stay mad at him. Besides, he never tried to be bad; he was just having fun being Stevie.

"Carole's friends begged her to go to the movies with them, but she said, 'No way! I have to help my cousin Marsha with her party!' Carole wants this party planned right down to the last salted peanut!" Marsha hooted into the phone. "Isn't she a scream?"

Collette felt like screaming. She did *not* want to go over to Marsha's while Carole Rambarski was there. Carole had had it in for Collette ever since Collette had accidentally gotten her in trouble by handing Mrs. Cessano a crumpled pack of cigarettes she'd found on the floor of the Cessano's Mercedes. Collette had thought they were Mrs. Cessano's.

They weren't.

Collette shivered as she remembered the hateful look Carole had shot her as soon as Mrs. Cessano had stopped her cross-examination.

It was the look of a gunfighter.

"So come on over and go to the mall with us!" begged Marsha. "My mom wants you to, so you'll be a good influence on the two crazy girls, me and Carole."

Once again Marsha and Carole laughed.

"I don't know," began Collette slowly. She was glad to see how dark it was getting outside. Mrs. Murphy didn't like Collette at the Ross Park Mall after dark without her.

Collette smiled, glad her mother would get her out of saying no. It was always much easier if a mom said no for you. No one got mad at other kids' moms.

Collette covered the phone with her hand.

"Marsha wants me to go to the mall with her and that cousin of hers. The one with the dyed black hair."

Mother was busy picking up bits of glass from the floor and only nodded her head with a faint grunt.

"It's the snooty one, the one that doesn't like me."

"Oh, great! Pick up a present for Marsha's birthday while you're there," suggested Mother. She stood, dropping the glass into the waste can. "Boy, this is working out fine. I was really dreading putting all the kids in the car tomorrow to buy that present."

Collette's heart sank.

"Can I go to the mall with you, Collette?" Laura tried to smooth down her shiny blonde bangs. "I'm still clean."

"Me, too!" added Stevie. He picked up the bottom of his sweatshirt and wiped the top layer of dirt from his face. "Look at how clean I am."

"No, now you children run downstairs and turn on the TV special. It's almost starting. I'll pop the corn and we'll have a party." Mother winked at Collette like she had just done her a big favor. "Collette wants to go have a little fun with her friends."

No, I don't, Collette wanted to shout.

Mother unzipped her wallet and handed Collette a ten-dollar bill. "Here, sweetie. Bring me my change."

Change? Collette stared at the ten dollars. She didn't want to be rude or hurt her mother's feelings, but there was nothing you could buy someone like Marsha for only ten dollars.

There wasn't a thing in Marsha's bedroom that cost less than twenty or thirty bucks. Even her stuffed animals came from Germany or France. They all had fancy names and real soft stuffing.

"Hey, Collette! Can you come?" Marsha was beginning to sound impatient.

Collette looked up at her mother, who was smiling and looking grateful that she didn't have to tear the kids away from Saturday morning cartoons.

"Yes, I guess so. . . ."

"Good, get over here. My mom has to return these geeky clown plates and napkins she bought for the party." Marsha snorted. "Or maybe I should just give them to you for *your* next party, Collette!"

Collette pulled the phone away from her ear and frowned. She was going to stick her tongue out, too, but her family was staring at her. She mumbled a good-bye and hung up instead.

"Can't I please, please, please, come?" begged Stevie. He folded his little hands together and followed Collette around the kitchen. "I will be so good."

"I am gooder than Stevie," insisted Laura. "And I really have to go, Mommy. All my school crayons have Stevie bite-marks in them."

Stevie grinned at Laura, raising both hands like a vampire and turning to stalk toward her. He stuck out his tongue.

"Get away from me, Stevie!" demanded Laura. She took a step closer to Collette. "Daddy says he's going to put you in your room the next time you lick me!"

"Mom, I don't know if I can find anything Marsha will like for ten dollars!"

Mother raised an eyebrow. "I think you can. In fact, I hope to have some change left." Mother smiled and brushed back Collette's blonde hair. "Keep the change and buy yourself something."

"Don't buy Marsha anything for her birthday," instructed Jeff. "She thinks she's so hot, just 'cause she's rich."

"Yeah," added Stevie. "Marsha is a bad guy, right, Jeff?"

"Give her mud!" laughed Jeff.

"Why don't you run upstairs and change into your new sweater with the white hearts?" suggested Mother.

"Why? I'm not trying to impress anyone." Collette frowned. Maybe it would be a good idea if she *did* impress people like Carole and Marsha. Then they wouldn't go out of their way to be so mean to her all the time.

"I want to go!" whined Stevie. He crossed his arms and blocked Collette's way out of the kitchen. "I won't yell or chase people or nothing if you take me."

"Get out of the way, Stevie," Mother said. But she was smiling and didn't really sound like she meant it. That was the trouble with Stevie. Nobody ever got mad at him and he was growing up all wrong.

Just like me, thought Collette miserably. Her parents were so busy with all the littler guys that they never stopped to check up on Collette to see if she was doing a good job of being ten years old. As long as she didn't suck her thumb or throw temper tantrums, they thought she was doing okay.

"Move, Stevie!" ordered Collette as she shoved him aside.

"Wow, what a grouch," muttered Jeff as he stepped clear of her.

Collette stormed up the stairs, madder than ever that Marsha ended up being right about so many things. Marsha always said the Murphy house was crazy. Collette's parents were so used to the noise and confusion, they didn't even try hard to change things. Too bad they never watched television shows where a ten-year-old daughter could just walk into a quiet den and find two parents sitting and waiting for a problem they could help their daughter solve.

Marsha had a family like that.

At the top of the stairs, Collette peered through

Jeff's open bedroom door. She could see Marsha's huge white house across the street, lights blazing from every window.

Collette stared at the lights, thinking. What if Marsha, Sarah, and the other girls in the fifth grade were right and Collette really was some kind of oddball? A baby who would never catch up with the rest of the girls her age?

She turned and raced down the stairs. Collette dreaded going to the mall almost as much as she dreaded the party tomorrow afternoon. But she had to go. Had to go to both to find out if she really was totally different from everyone else in the fifth grade. She didn't have a choice.

# Chapter Five

Collette shivered as she rang Marsha's front bell. The chimes inside the house seemed to go on forever.

"Door's unlocked. Come in, dear!" called Mrs. Cessano. As Collette walked in, she could see Marsha's mother leaning over the spiral staircase, her long red fingernails waving back and forth over the banister.

"My nails are still wet. Come on up, Collette. The girls are in Marsha's room having a positively *grand* time with all the party plans."

Collette smiled, but she took her time hanging up her coat on the fancy brass coatrack. She needed more time to prepare herself for Carole. Every time she came to Marsha's house Carole seemed older, taller, and more sure of herself.

As Collette opened Marsha's door, her eyes locked with Carole's immediately.

"Well, I was just telling Marsha that I bet you weren't coming to the mall with us, after all."

"It's about *time*," said Marsha as she closed the door behind Collette. "As soon as my mom finishes her nails, we're leaving."

Marsha ran over to her dresser and held up a Notre Dame pennant. "Isn't this great, and look . . ." Marsha unrolled a poster of a young man with purple hair and a custom-made guitar. "It's Grateful Zoomies . . . nice, huh?"

Collette nodded. The poster looked a lot like Stevie's posters of He-Man.

"And Carole brought her boyfriend's jacket over so I can leave it lying across my chair," continued Marsha. "It's a letter jacket, like the jocks all wear, right, Carole?"

Carole nodded, her gum cracking inside her mouth like kindling wood.

She stood up, pulling at her skintight jeans as she walked over to the chair. "Now the trick is to have it just kind of lying there. Don't plop it down in the center like you're trying to show it off. Be subtle . . . always be subtle."

Collette stared at Carole's short, black, spiky hair and the royal-blue eyeshadow outlining each green eye. Nothing about Carole was subtle.

"You aren't having the party up *here*, are you?" asked Collette. Marsha usually offered everyone a free tour of her house the first time they came over to play. She thought the whole world was just dying to know how special and fancy it was.

Carole shrugged, waving her hand around Marsha's room.

"Hey listen, you have to be ready for whatever, know what I mean? If I had a room like this, I sure would want to show it off. . . ." Carole stopped, then started to strut around the room like a squad leader. "Of course, things look pretty bad right now. Looks like a little nursery school, if you want my real opinion, Marsha."

Marsha crossed her arms and frowned at her room. "It looks awful!"

"Got to get rid of the kid stuff," ordered Carole with a quick snap of her gum. "Take that shelf, for example. All you need is Mr. Rogers standing in front of it with his tennis shoes, know what I mean?"

Marsha practically ran to the shelf, sweeping it clean with one swoop of her arm. Stuffed bunnies, small brown bears and miniature kitty cats bounced down to the carpet, ricocheting to all corners of the room.

"Marsha?" cried Collette, dodging to the left as a white unicorn flew by. "What are you doing?"

"I am trying to get this room ready for the party tomorrow," muttered Marsha, pausing to scowl at a large pink rabbit.

"I would hate to see *your* room, Collette," snorted Carole. "I bet you have one of those little night-lights in the shape of a balloon, don't you?"

Marsha's shoulders shook as she started to giggle.

Collette glared at Carole, refusing to get mad or start defending her room. Carole would never, ever, be invited over to see it.

"Beats me why you've kept these ratty little dust collectors around all these years, anyway, Marsha." Carole wore such a disgusted look on her face you would have thought she had just found week-old pizza on the shelves instead of beautiful stuffed animals and knickknacks.

Collette could tell Carole's comments were up-setting Marsha.

"Well, I certainly didn't ask people to buy me all this . . . this junk!" sniffed Marsha defensively.

Carole slumped into a chair and studied the room with a hopeless look on her face. "I just hope we can get it ready in time, that's all."

Marsha blew up both sides of her bangs before she turned and knocked off an entire family of white china mice from another shelf.

"Marsha, stop it!" cried Collette, rushing over to pick up Mother Mouse. "You broke her!" Col-lette cradled the small apron and tiny left ear in her hand. "And you knocked Father Mouse's whole head off. I can't even find his nose."

"Boo-hoo," snorted Carole, wiping fake tears from her cheeks. She strutted over to the dresser, bending down to comb her fingers through her jagged hair. "Poor widdle mouses!"

Marsha looked from Carole to Collette. She studied the small white figures scattered across her carpet.

"You didn't have to break them, Marsha," insisted Collette. She knelt to pick up all the pieces and laid them on the night stand. "I mean, if you don't want this stuff, give it to poor children, or . . . or save them until . . . until you like them again."

Marsha stood and pulled at her bangs. She glanced at the mice and finally shrugged.

"Atta girl," laughed Carole. She unrolled the guitar player and taped it onto the back of Marsha's door.

Collette watched Marsha's face. Why was she acting this way? Collette could still remember when Marsha's dad had given her the mouse family. He had them all lined up on the kitchen counter to greet her when she returned from her first day of kindergarten.

How could she treat them this way . . . just to impress someone like Carole?

"Pitch anything that makes you look like a big baby," advised Carole. She knocked the last raccoon and monkey from the top shelf and placed three of her own swimming trophies in a row. "Trophies, posters, pennants are all going to look a whole lot more grown-up than all this Mother Goose stuff."

Marsha nodded, eyeing her empty shelves.

Collette took the Kleenex box from the dresser and gently placed the pieces of the mouse family inside, carefully wrapping Mother Mouse in the pink tissue. "I'll take the mice home with me," said Collette quietly. "I'll glue them back together for my little sister."

"Oh, sure," hooted Carole, nudging Marsha. "You'll glue them and keep them for yourself, Collette. Who are you trying to kid?"

Not you, Collette wanted to shout. She bit the inside of her lip until the stinging stopped in her eyes. She pulled out another tissue and slowly wrapped Father Mouse's head. It was smaller than a jellybean, so perfectly painted that you could tell right away he was winking at you.

Carole tossed a panda bear across the room and clapped as it landed headfirst in the trash can. "You have to grow up sometime, girls. The sooner the better, too, or you'll be left behind. . . ." Carole brushed off her hands and rocked back and forth on her heels, studying the shelves. "Yup, left behind with the losers . . . the creeps who never fit in."

Carole turned as if in slow motion and stared at Collette. She may as well have said, ". . . like Collette Murphy!"

Collette tapped her fingers against the tissue box. She didn't wait for Marsha to stick up for her. Marsha wouldn't. Sarah would have, even against someone as mean as Carole.

At least Sarah would have last week. Before all this signpost business.

Collette jumped as Marsha's mother rapped on the door and then stuck her head in. She was all dressed up like she was going out for dinner. "Ready Freddie?" she joked. As she looked around the room, she frowned. "Marsha, it looks like a cyclone hit your room. Clean it up before the party, okay?"

Carole and Marsha looked at each other and laughed.

"I've been telling Marsha all evening she has to get her room ready for the party, Aunt Nancy," insisted Carole.

"Meet you out front, girls," Mrs. Cessano called as she started down the stairs.

Carole grabbed her jacket and kicked a calico cat under the bed as she raced out. "Last one in the car is a geek!"

Marsha opened her closet and pulled her jean jacket from the hanger.

"Marsha, do you want me to keep this stuff over at my house until your . . . your party is over?" offered Collette. Collette tried to keep her voice low so Carole wouldn't race back up the stairs to add her two-cents worth.

Marsha thought about it for a second, looking around the room. Probably testing herself to see if she was going to miss anything.

"No . . . no, I really think Carole is right. I've got to get rid of this stuff before my signpost party. It would probably bring bad luck if I brought it back in. . . ."

Collette nodded, but she didn't agree one bit.

But if Marsha didn't seem to mind getting rid of everything from her childhood, why should Collette care?

After all, Marsha's memories were scattered all over the floor, not hers.

Collette followed Marsha down the spiral staircase and out the front door. As Marsha raced down the front walk to the car, Collette shoved the tissue box with the mice family far, far under the tree by the side porch.

They would be safer there than in Marsha's room, where everything would end up in the trash.

As she ran to the car she could hear Carole declaring Collette to be last one in, the geek!

Collette took a deep breath of night air, wondering if Carole was right.

# Chapter Six

"Now then ladies, where shall we start?" asked Marsha's mother as she pulled off her leather gloves and looked around the mall.

Carole groaned. "Aunt Nancy, you aren't going to walk around the mall with us, are you?"

Marsha gave her mother a horrified gasp.

"Mom, you can't. Carole is a real teenager. What if some of her friends saw us?"

"It would be real geeky," mumbled Carole.

Mrs. Cessano looked at Marsha and gave a weak smile.

"I wouldn't be in the way, girls. I thought it might be kind of fun for all of us to get the party things."

Carole took charge.

"I'm just worried about Marsha, Aunt Nancy. You don't want her to get a reputation for being some kind of a nerd, do you?"

Mrs. Cessano turned pale. "Of course not. I want Marsha to be . . . well, popular and . . ."

"Mother," wailed Marsha. "I am not a little girl anymore. I am going to be eleven years old tomorrow. Don't you think I should be a little more independent, now that I am about to have my signpost?"

"You have a point," said Mrs. Cessano with a smile. "I don't want to stand in the way of a perfect signpost!"

Marsha and Carole gave each other a high five and started walking.

Mrs. Cessano turned and smiled at Collette.

"Dear, would you like to call your mother to see if she minds you walking around the mall without an adult? I know how she worries." Mrs. Cessano kept her voice low, but Carole heard it right away. She nudged Marsha and they both started to laugh.

Collette shoved her hands in her pockets and shook her head.

"I don't have to call. I've walked around the mall alone before. . . ."

Collette's cheeks grew hot as she realized that a lie could slip out as easily as the truth.

"Well then, it's settled," declared Mrs. Cessano. "I'll meet you in front of Waggoner's Variety Store in an hour."

She extended a small blue charge card toward Marsha. "Only charge two or three records and the paper plates."

"Thanks," said Marsha, shoving the card into her back jean pocket.

Collette watched Marsha's mother walk slowly down the upper level of the mall.

"Come here," ordered Carole, grabbing Marsha and Collette by the arm. "I have a surprise for you both."

Marsha all but squealed with excitement. "Tell me, Carole!"

Carole titled her head in the air, looking smug.

"By the time I am finished with you girls, you will look at least fourteen. Trust me."

Marsha beamed. "You're terrific!"

"What is it, Carole?" asked Collette. She

couldn't help herself, she was begining to get curious.

"I'll give you a clue," laughed Carole, tugging on Collette's blonde ponytail. "The moment your mothers see you, they'll notice."

Collette reached for her hair. It had taken her years to grow her hair this long. She wasn't going to cut it for Carole. She didn't even want to look fourteen.

"I'm not cutting my hair," cried Collette.

Carole laughed. "It's not your hair. In fact, come here. If you got rid of this silly ponytail, you would look great."

Without even asking, Carole reached over and pulled the rubber band from Collette's hair.

"Not bad," said Carole approvingly as she fluffed Collette's hair.

"You look good," added Marsha. She smiled at Collette, nodding her head.

Collette shook her hair out. She liked ponytails, but if wearing her hair a different way kept Carole off her back, then it was all right with her.

"Come on ladies, just a few more feet," said Carole as they turned the corner.

With a grand flourish she extended her arms.

"TA-DA!"

"An ear-piercing booth?" cried Marsha. "This is the surprise?"

"Yeah, I had mine pierced when I was nine, Marsha. You and Collette are way overdue."

"But this stuff hurts," moaned Marsha. She covered both ears with her hands.

"No way!" muttered Collette. Her mother said she had to wait until she was twelve to have them pierced.

"It only hurts for a second," said Carole. "It isn't major surgery, Marsha!"

The ear-piercing girl leaned over the counter. She stopped chewing her gum long enough to study Carole.

"So what's it gonna be, kid?"

Carole's lips curled up into a tight little knot. Collette could tell she really disliked being called a kid.

"I don't know, Carole," began Marsha. She and Collette took a step back.

"Trust me, Marsha. This will be the all-time *best* signpost symbol in our family history," Carole insisted. "Let's face it, some signposts just don't last. Your mom can't wear her signpost anymore. Aunt

67

Helen had that five-foot ice sculpture of her initials . . . that melted. No one in our whole family has had a good, lasting signpost symbol. . . . You'll be the first."

Collette could tell by Marsha's silly smirk that she like the idea of being the first with something important.

"What was your signpost, Carole?" asked Collette.

Carole looked embarrassed.

"Oh, it wasn't all that hot. My mom picked it."

"What was it?" persisted Collette.

Carole actually shuddered. "My mom hired some old guy to paint my portrait. I look like a real creep. My hair was in these stupid-looking curls, no makeup . . . really gross."

Carole tugged on Marsha's arm, shaking her. "You should be thankful you have me, Marsha. I'm older so I've been through it all before. If you get your ears pierced, it will last forever!"

"But it will hurt!" groaned Marsha. "I hate pain!"

Collette slid onto a bench by the booth. She was glad signposts didn't run in her family.

"We are running a special if you kids is in-teres-ted!" announced the girl as she drummed her long fingernails on the counter.

The girl tapped out a tune with her nails for awhile, then stopped to pull a large wad of pink gum from her mouth.

TWANG!!!

She pitched it neatly into a metal trashcan.

"Bull's-eye, second this week. It helps to have a good eye in my line of work."

Marsha slid onto the bench beside Collette.

"Hey, don't worry, kid," laughed the girl as she twisted slowly around on her metal stool. "I haven't botched up an ear yet. Heard about a girl over at Northway Mall, though. She sneezed at the wrong moment and YE-OW! That girl sneezed herself right out of a job!"

Marsha leaned closer to Collette, her hands protecting her ears.

"Don't go chicken on me," growled Carole, pointing her finger at Marsha. Carole waved a twenty-dollar bill at the piercing girl. "Is this enough?"

Leaning over the edge of the booth, the girl squinted and sized Collette and Marsha up.

"Both of ya getting done?"

Collette shook her head. With a gentle push she shoved Marsha forward.

"It's her signpost!"

The piercing girl sat back down on her stool, studying her nails and flicking bits of orange polish high into the air.

"You look kinda young to me. If you ain't sixteen, you need a note from your parents."

"Good." Collette sighed in pure relief. Now they could go get the paper plates and records.

"We have a note," announced Carole. She said it so smoothly you would have sworn it was the truth.

Marsha's hand shot out, her fingers digging into Collette's wrist.

"You do it, too, Collette," pleaded Marsha in a shaky voice. "It will be kind of fun if we do it together."

Collette frowned. Pain was never fun, no matter how many people were involved.

"Give us a minute to talk," explained Carole in a rush. She grabbed Marsha and Collette and shoved them away from the booth.

"Okay, now listen up, you two," whispered Carole. She glanced over her shoulder as she searched her pockets for a pen and scrap of paper. "Now, I'll write you both a note. I'll write Collette's with my left hand, Marsha's with my right. That girl is so dumb, she'll never know the difference."

Collette cleared her throat. She'd better jump in now and tell Carole that she was not going to get her ears pierced with a forged note.

Carole used the railing as a writing surface and quickly scribbled a note with her right hand. "Now the important thing to remember when you lie is not to act rushed. When the girl asks for your permission slip, just reach in your pocket, slow as can be, and hand her the note like it's no big deal."

Marsha took her note, folding it carefully. Her eyes never left Carole's. She nodded her head up and down like she was receiving life-saving information.

Collette watched as Carole wrote the second note with her left hand. She bit her lip. Lying was wrong. But lying on paper was even worse.

It was probably some sort of crime.

Carole extended the note to Collette. "Here," she said, waving it up and down in front of Collette's hand.

"No," said Collette. She didn't want to say anything else. Carole would only ignore her.

Carole let the note fall to the floor. "Didn't think you would go through with it, Goldilocks. Boy, am I glad you aren't my cousin."

Carole shoved the pen back into her pocket and pushed Marsha toward the booth.

"Come on, Cuz, it's signpost time."

Marsha walked slowly, her chin drooping with each step.

"So what kind of earrings do you want me to load in the gun?" asked the girl as she read the permission slip.

Marsha shuddered at the mention of the word "gun."

"Gee . . . I like those," she said. Marsha seemed to be getting some of her color back as she pointed to a large set of pearl earrings.

"You're looking at thirty bucks, kid," stated the girl. She gave Collette a lopsided grin as though she really loved shocking people with prices.

"Thirty bucks," repeated Marsha.

Carole groaned. "Pick something else, Marsha. I only have twenty."

Marsha studied the glass case, then pointed her finger at the smaller earrings. She tapped the glass and smiled hopefully.

"How about the gold balls? They aren't so big."

"Twenty-nine for the big ones, twenty-two for the medium, and only fifteen bucks for the shrimpy little ones. Most kids like yourself pick the shrimps on account of them being so cheap and all."

Collette watched as Marsha and Carole exchanged identical scowls. Their families probably took an oath at birth, swearing they would never buy the cheapest of anything in life.

Carole searched through her wallet, frowning as though it had deliberately eaten an extra twenty-dollar bill.

"So, which earrings do you want?" asked the girl.

Carole bent her wallet back and forth as she studied the display case. "The shrimpy — er, the small gold balls," she said slowly.

Marsha leaned her elbows on the counter and sighed.

"Gee, Carole . . . I don't know. I mean, you are

being so nice to me to get this for my birthday. But I think the gold balls are just a little too . . . well, little."

"They aren't *that* little," interrupted Carole.

"Sure they are, Carole. Look at them. Balls of gold that small are the kind some people stick in their babies' ears when they are only two hours old."

Collette wanted to shake Marsha.

"Don't get mad, Carole, but what if I jinx my signpost by starting it off in a cheap way?"

Carole nodded. Signposts must be very serious things in their families.

The piercing girl was windexing the counter-top, looking as bored as Collette felt. Collette swallowed a yawn.

Suddenly Carole brightened.

"Hey, wait a minute. Collette, in the car you said your mom gave you money to get Marsha a birthday present, right?"

Everyone, including the piercing girl, turned to stare at Collette, waiting.

"It's only ten dollars."

"Sold!" snapped Carole, her hand dropping down like a railroad crossing bar.

Collette stood frozen, staring at Carole's out-stretched hand.

"Well, . . . I think my mom was expecting me to bring home something we could wrap up and put a bow on. . . ." stammered Collette.

"Give me a break!" exploded Carole. She socked herself in the forehead with her fist. "Don't you ever, ever in your life do anything without worrying what your mommy or daddy will think about it, Collette? I thought you were supposed to be the class genius or something."

The piercing girl snickered.

Turning her back on Carole, Collette looked into her wallet and pulled out the money. She handed it to Marsha. "Happy Birthday."

"Thanks," said Marsha quickly, slapping the money down on the counter.

Collette busied herself with closing her wallet so she didn't have to look at anyone.

Then she walked to the railing, looking down at all the fun places she usually visited when she came to the mall.

Behind her she could hear Carole coaxing Marsha to get into the chair. Marsha was beginning to sound whiny now.

Collette sighed.

No matter what she said right now, Marsha and Carole would ignore it. No one really thought Collette had any good ideas outside of schoolwork.

Besides, Marsha only cared about Carole's opinion right now.

Collette bent down and rested her chin on her hands, watching people lining up to buy ice cream.

The peacefulness of the scene was almost hypnotizing until Collette heard the scream.

# Chapter Seven

The pitch of the scream was so high it could have only come from one person: Marsha!

"Marsha!" cried Collette as she tore across the mall. "Are you all right?"

"Does it look like I'm all right?" sputtered Marsha, using both hands to wipe away the tears. "My earlobe was almost ripped away."

"Well, it was your fault for jerking your head away like that," scolded the girl, dabbing at the blood with a cotton swab. "Now let's just wait a sec till the blood lets up and I'll give this earlobe another shot."

"Oh, no, you won't," shouted Marsha, grabbing onto Collette's arm with full force.

"You can't walk around with one pierced ear,"

said Carole. "You'll look like some sort of a pirate."

Collette patted Marsha on the back to let her know that she was still there.

"I'd just let the hole grow in, Marsha. In a month, no one will even know it was there."

"Are you crazy?" snapped Marsha. "I didn't go through all this pain for nothing."

Collette sighed. It was hard to comfort someone as stubborn as Marsha!

"Make up your mind, kid. You can't sit on this stool all day," reminded the piercing girl. "I'm expectin' the after-dinner crowd any minute. Do you want me to try again or what?"

"Let me think. . . . Just let me think for a minute," wailed Marsha, squirming miserably on the stool.

Carole leaned over the booth and gave Marsha a quick smack on the leg.

"For cryin' out loud, let's get this thing over with. She isn't trying to take out your appendix. Stop acting like a big baby."

"I'm not," insisted Marsha, touching her earlobe and searching for blood. "But when you lose as much blood as I just did, your thinking gets a little fuzzy, that's all."

"Well, unfuzz it real quick, because I'm getting real bored, real fast," growled Carole.

Reaching out, Collette gave Marsha a gentle pat, reminding her that she was still on her side in case she wanted to tell Carole to go mind her own business.

"Listen, Marsha," said Carole in a more gentle tone. "If you get the other ear pierced, I'll spring for a new pair of earrings for you!"

"Really?" cried Marsha. "Can I get a pair of real gold hoops like yours?"

"I ain't got all day," sighed the piercing girl as she banged a few drawers shut with her foot.

"I thought you only had twenty dollars," pointed out Collette.

Carole silenced Collette with a sneer.

"Gold hoops, think how great they would look at the party . . ." whispered Carole with a tempting smile.

"Okay," mumbled Marsha, closing her eyes and squeezing all of the blood from Collette's hand.

"That's it," said the girl, putting a back on each ear. "Come back in twenty minutes and I'll tighten the backs for you."

Marsha hopped from the stool, examining her ears in the small mirror.

"I did it, I can't believe I did it."

"You look at least twelve years old now," commented Carole approvingly.

"What happened to fourteen?" asked Marsha, looking hurt.

"You're a little short for fourteen," Carole replied.

"Now let's get the gold hoops," reminded Marsha. "I am really getting excited about this party."

"I thought we used all the money, Carole," reminded Collette.

Carole laughed. "I have a very special charge card. We won't be using money."

Marsha linked arms with Collette and Carole.

"This has been so much fun. I feel older already. I'm glad you talked me into having my ears pierced, Carole."

Carole stopped in front of Boss's Jewelry Store. With its green awnings and elaborate brass handles, it was the fanciest store in the mall.

"In here?" gasped Collette. Her mother had never been brave enough to take four children to such an elegant store.

"Step inside, ladies," laughed Carole. She held open the heavy wooden door for them.

Wow, thought Collette, suddenly breathless. The store was so beautiful. Her feet sank into the thick beige carpeting. Soft music was floating through the air like mist.

"Are you sure you're allowed to charge something in here?" whispered Collette. "Everything in here must cost a thousand dollars."

"You just have to know how to shop," giggled Carole. "Relax and do whatever I tell you to."

Collette smiled, beginning to relax at last. This trip to the mall was turning out to be fun.

After all, here she was in Boss's, the nicest store in the mall.

A woman with silver hair came up beside them.

"May I help you ladies with something?"

"I want a pair of gold hoop earrings, like hers," replied Marsha, pointing to Carole's ears.

The lady studied the earrings and smiled.

"I think the department stores carry that line of costume jewelry. . . ."

"We're just looking, thanks," said Carole briskly as she steered Marsha away.

Marsha's mouth fell open.

"Carole, you promised me a pair of earrings. I was so brave — "

"Shhhh," hissed Carole. "You'll get your earrings, but I don't want that nosy saleslady hanging around."

Looking around the store, Collette smiled. What did Carole think this was, a self-service jewelry store?

Marsha stopped in front of a caddy filled with silver and gold earrings.

"Look at these," she cried. "I love these!"

Collette flipped the card over.

"Seventy-five dollars . . . wow, and they aren't even solid gold."

Carole frowned. "All the real solid stuff is locked up. Pick a pair from the caddy."

Marsha nodded, slowly turning the circle.

"Hoops!"

"One hundred and fifteen dollars," squeaked Collette. Not even Carole would charge that much for someone's birthday.

How rich could anyone be?

"Are these too much?" asked Marsha with a pout.

Carole shook her head.

"Just make sure you want them because I can't return them."

"Why not?" asked Collette. Boss's was a lovely store. They would probably be nice about a return.

"I can't . . ." hissed Carole.

"Ask her to gift wrap them . . . tell her it's my birthday," said Marsha.

Carole snatched the earrings from Marsha, her good mood beginning to cloud over.

"No gift wrapping."

Marsha began to pull on her bangs.

"How about a box?"

"No," Carole snapped in a hoarse whisper.

Collette studied Carole's face. Why in the world was she getting so upset? Surely Boss's wouldn't mind giving Carole a box after she bought a hundred-dollar pair of earrings.

"Honestly!" exploded Carole. "You two are the dumbest kids I've ever met."

Red flooded Marsha's face. She stared at her fingernails.

"What's so dumb?" asked Collette. Maybe this was her first time in Boss's, but the rules here couldn't be that different than in other stores.

"Let's get the saleslady. We have to get back to

the ear-piercing booth before we meet your mom, Marsha," reminded Collette.

Carole slapped her hand to her forehead.

"Keep your mouth shut, Goldilocks, or you'll ruin everything."

Collette took a step back. Carole was snapping orders like some sort of a drill sergeant.

"We have to meet her mother in ten minutes," repeated Collette.

Marsha drummed her fingers on the glass case.

"What's wrong, Carole? Collette's right."

Carole dangled the earrings in front of Marsha's face.

"Do you want these or not?"

"Of course I do," said Marsha.

"Then let me do it my way," said Carole, closing her hand around them. "You two go over and ask the saleslady to show you a gold charm bracelet. She'll have to unlock the case for that. . . . I'll get the earrings and meet you outside."

Marsha looked puzzled.

"Who wants a charm bracelet?"

Carole crossed her eyes and groaned.

"Let's get out of here, Marsha," said Collette quickly, pulling Marsha by the elbow.

"What?" said Marsha loudly.

"Shhh . . ." hissed Carole. Looking right at Collette, she sneered.

"Well, bingo. Smarty-pants here finally figured out how my charge card works."

Collette glared right back at Carole.

"Carole doesn't charge, she steals. . . ."

Marsha's eyes widened.

Together Marsha and Collette watched as Carole put her clenched fist in her jacket pocket. When she withdrew it, the earrings were gone.

"TA-DA!" Carole whispered. "Happy Birthday, Marsha!"

Collette's head shot up, searching for the saleslady. Surely somebody saw Carole. Stealing couldn't be that easy.

Carole leaned over and casually turned the earring caddy. Stopping it, she pulled some large silver balls from the rack.

"Get these for me, Marsha. I'll wear them to your party."

Marsha stared at the earrings on the glass counter. She licked and relicked her lips.

"Let's leave," urged Collette, walking a few steps away. "This is stupid."

"You do want me to come to your party, Marsha, don't you?" whispered Carole.

Marsha nodded, her eyes still glued to the silver balls.

"Stop it," said Collette loudly. "Let's get out of here."

Carole reached over and pinched her arm.

"You ruin this and you'll be sorrier than you've ever been."

Tears glistened in Collette's eyes. Her arm stung, but the real pain was coming from deep inside.

Things were so confusing. It was almost like a bad movie they would show you in school about lying and stealing. When the film was almost over they would stop it and say, "All right now, boys and girls, what would you do in a situation like this?"

"Charge them," ordered Carole, staring a hole straight through Marsha's head.

Shifting her weight to the right and left, Collette waited. But waited for what? Marsha did anything Carole asked. And if the three of them stood here much longer, they would all be caught.

"I'm leaving," she announced, turning and

marching across the carpet to the door.

With her hand on the smooth brass handle, she paused. Any minute she would see Marsha standing beside her and the two of them could walk out.

Any minute now. . . .

The music drifted, surrounding Collette as she stood frozen at the door. Her hand closed around the remaining dollar in her pocket. She could run out right now and buy some glue to fix Marsha's china mice.

She didn't have to stay here. She could walk out right now.

After all, Marsha wasn't even her best friend.

Collette shivered in the warm room. With a final glance over her shoulder she saw Marsha standing beside Carole, pushing the earrings slowly back and forth on the smooth counter.

Marsha didn't know what to do. She didn't even know how to get away from Carole so she could decide.

Spinning around, Collette half ran to Marsha.

"Marsha, quick. . . . your mom is here for us!"

Marsha covered her mouth with her hands and raced to the door. Collette grabbed her by the arm and propelled her out into the corridor.

"Where?" cried Marsha, her voice shaking. "Where's my mom?"

Collette pushed Marsha against the railing, her eyes beginning to sting with tears.

"Nowhere, you dummy. I just wanted to get you out of there. What's wrong with you? Are you crazy to even think — ?"

Marsha pushed Collette's hand from her arm.

"You lied! Carole is going to kill us!" Boss's door swung open quickly.

Carole shot out like a cannonball, her eyes narrowed to angry slits.

"You creeps! I hate you . . . I hate you both!"

Marsha shoved Collette out of her way as she ran to stand next to Carole.

"She lied, Carole. . . . She. . . ."

Raising her fist high in the air, Carole began a slow march toward Collette.

"You make me sick, Miss Goody-two-shoes. . . ."

Stepping backwards, Collette felt the railing against her. She didn't even care if Carole hit her, she felt so bruised already.

Marsha was right. She must be too young for the fifth grade because she was suddenly totally confused by everyone. Collette suddenly needed a new set of directions just to understand her old friends.

"That's her!" shrieked a voice.

Whistles blew and suddenly adults were swarming around them.

Startled, Collette jerked her head around the angry circle.

From between Marsha and Carole, Collette's eyes locked with the saleslady from Boss's.

"There they are," the saleslady cried, pointing her ballpoint pen in the air like a sword. "Grab them!"

As if on cue, the heavyset security guard, his face rigid, walked toward them.

Marsha's hand reached out and clasped Collette's as he drew nearer, his handcuffs and billy club dancing wildly from his belt.

Collette closed her eyes, but it did no good. She could still see the saleslady barking out her last command.

"Arrest the thieves! Arrest them all!"

# Chapter Eight

"I'm innocent!" squealed Marsha as the guard walked toward her.

"Go on, all three of you, back inside the store," barked the security guard. Pointing to Carole with his billy club, he motioned to the entrance of the store. "You first, Miss. You are the leader of this little band, aren't you?"

"Get away from me," cried Carole, her face twisted into a scowl. "We didn't do anything."

"I became suspicious as soon as they refused my offer of assistance," announced the saleslady. "They said they were just looking. . . ." She paused to give a short laugh. "Just looking, indeed!"

The guard got behind them, herding the three into the store like a large, angry sheepdog.

Collette narrowed her eyes, trying to blur her surroundings as she reentered the store. She didn't want to look at any of the customers who were probably just standing still, waiting to catch a glimpse of the thieves.

I didn't do a thing . . . not a single thing, Collette wanted to shout to them all.

They followed the saleslady into a cramped back room, already crowded with boxes and type-writers.

"I didn't take the silver earrings," wailed Marsha miserably. "They should still be on the counter, where I left them."

"Shut up, Marsha," snapped Carole. "Don't tell them a thing!"

Suddenly Carole lowered her face in her hands and began to cry. Her shoulders shook as each fresh sob broke through.

It was hard to swallow, watching Carole cry so hard. Collette watched for a second, then looked away. It was too painful to see anyone as scared as Carole must be.

The earrings had to be in her pocket, just where she put them. Had she tossed in the silver pair after Marsha left the store?

"I want you girls to empty out your pockets," ordered the saleslady, crossing her arms and leaning against the closed door.

You could tell how angry she was. Her voice was low and practically shaking with rage.

Carole began to cry louder than ever. She probably wanted to drown out the saleslady's request.

"I didn't take anything," whimpered Marsha. Digging deep into her jeans, she began making a small pile of gum wrappers, tissues, and a half-eaten pack of Lifesavers.

She paused when she pulled out her mother's blue charge card. Her lips began to quiver as she gazed at the card.

Collette shook her head. Poor Marsha. Seeing the charge card was a big reminder that her mother was going to hear all about this.

The security guard reached in his pocket and pulled out a small spiral notebook and pencil.

"Okay. First of all, how old are you girls?"

"Ten," shouted Marsha. "I'm only ten years old!"

With the stubby end of his pencil, the guard pointed to Collette.

"What about you, Blondie?"

Tears flashed across Collette's eyes. She blinked them away. She was starting to feel more mad than scared, now. She had not done a thing, and she didn't deserve to be in this messy little room with two angry adults.

"My name is Collette Murphy. I am ten years old and I didn't take a thing from your store."

Reaching into her pocket, she tossed her wrinkled dollar bill onto the scratched table top.

The saleslady gave a disappointed sigh as she stared at the tabletop. No jewelry.

"Well, I wasn't sure about you two, but I did see this girl put something into her pocket. I saw her with my very own eyes."

"How old are you?" asked the guard, leaning toward Carole.

Carole looked up, wiping her eyes with the hem of her sweater. Two crooked streams of black makeup dribbled down her cheeks.

"She's only thirteen," cried Marsha. "Carole, wipe off your makeup and show them."

Carole reached in her pocket and tossed the earrings onto the table.

"I wasn't going to steal them. I only took them outside to ask my friends if I should buy them."

The guard rubbed the pencil against the side of his nose and laughed.

"Sure you did. . . . What's your name?"

Carole slid back in her chair and crossed her arms. She gave the guard her best scowl. "I don't have to tell you anything."

"I'm calling the police," said the saleslady, her voice beginning to rise. "I am sick to death of shoplifters. . . ." She picked up the phone.

"Wait, wait. . . ." said Collette. "Don't call them yet. Her name is Carole Rambarski."

"You creep!" shouted Carole, standing.

"Holy cow, Collette," whispered Marsha.

Collette felt like screaming. Did Marsha and Carole think they were just going to walk out of the jewelry store without going through all this?

"We came to the mall with Mrs. Cessano. Could you please have her paged?"

The saleslady nodded, picking up the phone and pressing a button. Glancing up, she gave Collette a gentle smile.

But Collette didn't smile back. It was too late for the lady to try and be nice to her now. She had already made her feel like a thief.

After the call was made, the five of them sat in

silence until Mrs. Cessano burst through the door.

As soon as Carole saw her aunt, she began to sob all over again.

"Aunt Nancy," she cried, rising from her chair and rushing to her. "It's all a big mistake."

"Of course it is," assured Marsha's mother, patting Carole on the back and glaring at the large security guard.

"A mistake?" choked the guard. "We caught her running out of the store with earrings in her pocket. No receipt, no bag . . . no nothing!"

"Carole is my niece," stated Mrs. Cessano, as though that alone should explain everything. "She is not a common thief!"

"Yeah," added Marsha. She took a step closer to the guard. "She didn't mean to steal them."

"I'm sure she had every intention of coming back inside the store to pay for them," continued Mrs. Cessano.

"I only wanted to show them to Marsha, first," inserted Carole.

"Spare me the details," yawned the guard. "I've heard a hundred stories, a hundred times."

Turning to the saleslady, he said, "Do you want me to call the police now?"

"Oh, Aunt Nancy, help me," wailed Carole.

Mrs. Cessano dug inside her purse and pulled out her wallet.

"Let's forget the police. Carole is only thirteen years old. Let's see if we can settle this like adults. . . . Now I am willing to pay for the earrings."

Turning to the saleslady, Mrs. Cessano forced a smile. "Exactly how much were the earrings?"

"One hundred and twenty-five dollars," the lady answered. "With tax, of course."

"What?" shrieked Mrs. Cessano, sinking to a stool. "What were you girls doing even *looking* at such an expensive pair of earrings?" Mrs. Cessano waved one hand around the room. "I can't believe you even came into Boss's Jewelry Store. It's much too expensive for the three of you."

The tightness in Collette's throat began to loosen. Maybe if Marsha's mother got a little bit madder, the truth would be forced out.

"Answer me, Marsha, Carole," insisted Mrs. Cessano. She picked up the earrings and flashed them in front of Carole's face like a detective's badge. "Why did you have these in your pocket, Carole?"

"Aunt Nancy, I knew how upset you were that

Marsha couldn't use your signpost," began Carole. She stared at Marsha, nodding her head with each word. She probably wanted to send Marsha a message like, Whatever I say is our story, so go along with it! "So I got all the money I had been saving and decided to buy Marsha something that would be really special. I knew that would cheer you both up."

Carole gave her aunt a small, brave smile.

Mrs. Cessano was not smiling back. She studied the earrings, flipping them over and looking shocked all over again at the price.

"But Marsha couldn't even wear these, Carole. They're for pierced ears!"

All heads, even the security guard's, turned to Marsha. Marsha hung her head, letting her black hair cover each ear.

"Marsha Cessano!" her mother shouted. "What have you done to your ears?"

Marsha's shoulders began to shake as she started to cry. "I didn't want to do it," she sobbed. "It really hurt and I almost fainted."

Carole was chewing her bottom lip now, beginning to look more and more nervous. "Well, I suggested it, Aunt Nancy. But I didn't have enough money, so Collette insisted I take ten dollars."

Collette's heart stopped as she felt herself being drawn into the problem. Carole was going to twist the whole story around, making it sound like Collette had financed the whole event.

But Mrs. Cessano was pointing her finger at Carole. "What do you mean you didn't have enough money for the piercing? If you didn't have money for that, how in the world were you going to pay for these?"

Mrs. Cessano tossed the earrings down in front of Carole. They slid across the scratched tabletop and onto Carole's lap.

"You have a lot of explaining to do, Carole!" barked Mrs. Cessano. She pulled out her wallet, then gave an irritated sigh as she put it back and yanked out her checkbook. She scribbled a check with an angry flourish and handed it to the saleslady.

"Thank you . . ." Mrs. Cessano stopped, and for one terrible moment Collette thought Marsha's mother was going to burst into tears. "Thank you for being so nice about all of this," Mrs. Cessano finished.

"Nice?" sputtered Carole. She stood up and shoved both hands on her hips. "There was not one *nice* thing about them, Aunt Nancy. They said I tried to steal — "

Mrs. Cessano reached out and grabbed Carole's arm. "Shut up, Carole!"

Collette could see the security guard cover his smile as she followed the stiff, silent group out of the office and through the store.

"Mom, don't blame me. I was only trying to make my signpost special," insisted Marsha.

"If I hear the word signpost one more time, I will scream," hissed Mrs. Cessano between clenched teeth.

Collette and the security guard exchanged looks.

As they walked out into the night air, Collette shivered. Nothing had gone right tonight. It had been one awful event after the other.

The only good part of the whole evening was that now Collette wouldn't have to listen to any more talk about the signpost party.

After tonight's trip to the mall, there wasn't going to be any party!

# Chapter Nine

The shrill ringing of the phone fit into Collette's dream so perfectly, she didn't even stir. The ringing became the piercing whine of police cars as they drove right into the mall, sped up the escalators and surrounded Boss's Jewelry Store.

"Send out Carole and her two assistant thieves or we're sending the stink bombs in!" a policeman shouted through the megaphone.

Collette tossed her head back and forth.

"No . . . no, wait. I . . ."

They tossed the stink bomb anyway . . . a large, heavy one that landed right smack in the middle of her stomach.

Collette couldn't move . . . she couldn't get away!

"Collette! Wake up!"

Blinking, trying to pry open each eyelid, Collette focused on Laura. Laura, all snuggly soft in her yellow fuzzy sleeper, was lying across Collette's stomach.

"Hi, Collette!" Laura pointed to a large red ribbon tied around a ponytail on top of her head. "Like my new hair? I did it all by myself."

"It's nice, Laura," Collette yawned.

Laura rolled off Collette and scrambled under the covers beside her. "The telephone is for you. It's only Marsha. She called two times before this time."

Tossing back the covers, Collette scrambled out. Sunlight filled the bedroom. Boy, she really must have slept a long time.

Last night had been exhausting. First, all the bad things that happened at the mall and then having to come home and tell her mother and dad about it.

Her parents had been great. They even put all the other kids to bed first so the talk could be private for a change.

Never once had her parents asked if Collette had stolen anything. Daddy had said, "I trust you."

Collette picked up the phone and sat on the edge of her mother's bed.

"Hello?" She tried not to yawn into the phone.

"It's about time you woke up." Marsha sounded upset. "Can you meet me on my side porch, right now?"

Collette leaned back against her mother's large pillows. There was no way she wanted to go over to Marsha's house this morning. Marsha had been so rude on the trip home from the mall, sitting up front and crying the whole way home, blabbing her side of the story to her mother.

"Why can't you be more like Collette?" Marsha's mother had demanded last night. She drummed her fingernails against the steering wheel, frowning at Carole in the rearview mirror. "You don't see Collette Murphy piercing her ears with a forged note, shoplifting in the most expensive store in the mall — "

"Collette gave me the money to pierce my ears," Marsha had blurted out. "She said it was my birthday present!"

"I'm sure that wasn't her idea!" Mrs. Cessano had snapped.

Collette had felt angry all over again. Marsha wasn't a real friend at all.

"Can you come?" pleaded Marsha. "I really have to talk to you."

"I just got up. I haven't even had breakfast yet," said Collette slowly. "Maybe later. . . ."

"Collette, don't be mad at me," whined Marsha. "Everyone over here is already mad enough for the whole world."

Collette heard a small sniff at the other end.

"And today *is* my birthday," reminded Marsha quietly.

With a deep sigh, Collette nodded into the phone. She probably should try to be nice to Marsha today. Not only was it her birthday, but she had to spend it without a signpost party.

She didn't want to forgive Marsha so easily. But since the signpost party was canceled, she probably could go over and see what she wanted to talk about.

"I'll be over in ten minutes," Collette finally said.

"Thanks," said Marsha softly. "I'll be waiting on the swing."

After a quick breakfast, Collette ran down the driveway and across the street.

Marsha was sitting on the white wicker swing, pushing herself back and forth with her foot. She looked up, trying to look as pitiful as she could. Her eyes were puffy and red from crying. Each earlobe was painted red.

"Gosh, Marsha! What happened to your ears? They look terrible."

"My mom put iodine on them so they wouldn't get infected. And she says that she is going to put it on every day for a whole month."

Collette giggled.

"It isn't funny," said Marsha, suddenly tearful all over again. "I look like a clown."

Sitting down on the swing next to her, Collette stopped smiling. She had to admit that she had never seen Marsha so sad.

"Happy birthday," said Collette.

Marsha moaned before she buried her face in her hands.

"Hey . . . sorry," said Collette quickly. "I was only trying to get your mind off your clown ears!"

Marsha sobbed louder.

"I know how bad you must feel. I mean, you really got in a lot of trouble last night, but it's still a shame your mom got so mad at you."

Taking a small floral pillow from the swing, Marsha wiped the tears from her face.

"Mad isn't the word. She is livid, actually livid over everything. She said . . . she said that she is so dis-a-ppoint-ed. . . ." Marsha paused to swallow back the tears.

Staring off into space, Marsha shook her head.

"I've been crying all night. . . . Nothing will ever be the same at my house."

"Sure it will," said Collette, trying to make her voice as cheerful as possible. "Your parents could never stay mad at you."

"They said that Carole is a bad influence on me. And my mom won't let Carole come over again until she pays her back the hundred and twenty-five dollars . . . Carole has to work at her dad's hardware store after school to earn the money."

"Well, that sounds fair to me," said Collette honestly.

"And I had to put all my stuffed animals back on my shelves. . . ." Marsha curled her feet under her and slumped against Collette. "It doesn't even seem like my birthday. The birthday I've waited my whole life for. . . ."

"It's a shame your mom canceled your signpost party," said Collette softly. She tried to keep her voice as sad as possible, for Marsha's sake.

"She didn't cancel it."

"What?" Collette hopped off the swing so quickly it banged against the wall.

"But of course she canceled it," insisted Collette. "You snuck off and pierced your ears without telling her, then you almost got arrested in a jewelry store for stealing. . . ." Collette stopped for breath, wondering what else she could add to the list. "You broke your mouse family just to make some sort of teenage room!"

"My mom said the party is still on. She said it wouldn't be fair to spoil everyone else's fun, just because . . . because . . . I'm a dis-a-ppointment!"

A solitary tear rolled down Marsha's cheek.

"She didn't cancel the party?" repeated Collette.

Marsha nodded. "But I'm not going."

Collette flopped back onto the swing.

"I refuse to have my signpost," stated Marsha. "No one can force me to go to the party, either."

106

They both sat in silence, listening to the next-door neighbor trying to start his lawnmower.

If Marsha refused to go to the party, Mrs. Cessano would have to cancel it eventually. No one would want to go to a birthday party without the birthday person.

Collette realized that she wouldn't have to worry about the party anymore. One way or the other, it wouldn't happen. For some reason, it made her feel funny.

"My mom said that I would be the first person in her family to miss their signpost in almost a hundred years. . . ."

"That's a long time," agreed Collette.

"I'm not going, and that's final."

Collette leaned back in the swing. She suddenly felt sorry for Marsha. "It's up to you."

Marsha nodded.

"Of course, any decision you make will be pretty permanent. . . ."

Marsha looked up. "What do you mean?"

Collette pointed to the side door. "I can see your mom's new video camera inside. She'll take it to the party to record your signpost, but you won't be in it. . . ."

Marsha shrugged. "So what?"

"Well, at first I thought your party sounded dumb."

"You *sure* did," said Marsha. She stared at Collette. "Do you think it's still a dumb idea?"

"No . . . now I know how much it must mean to your mom. If she's still having it after all that trouble last night, it must mean a lot to her. And if it means this much to her, then it will probably mean that much to you when you're a mom."

Marsha shuddered. "It's hard to believe we'll ever be that old!"

Both girls were silent, pushing the swing with their feet.

"Carole isn't allowed to come to the party," Marsha said at last.

"Good."

Marsha giggled. "She really is . . . well . . . mean about some things, isn't she?"

"Must be all those hormones she has and I don't," joked Collette.

"But I still wish she could come," said Marsha seriously. "I talked to Sarah about it for over an hour this morning. She is so disappointed that Carole isn't coming to the party."

108

Collette's mouth fell open, shocked. "Why would Sarah care about your cousin? Sarah has never even met Carole."

And obviously Sarah never heard that Carole smokes, steals, and enjoys making fun of people.

"You see, Carole is a real teenager. She knows exactly what to say to boys. That's why I wanted her to help me. I've never done this before."

Carole didn't know everything in the whole world, Collette thought. She probably wouldn't know what to say to a single fifth-grade boy except, "Oh, aren't you short!" and "I can't believe you are wearing that geeky shirt!"

"Sarah is so worried that everyone will be too shy," continued Marsha. "Sarah feels sick, absolutely sick about the whole thing."

Collette nodded. She had felt the same sick feeling for a week.

"So Sarah and I decided that maybe you could help out a little at the party, Collette. Since it was practically your fault that Carole got caught."

"What?" Collette picked up a small pillow from the swing and whacked Marsha in the arm. "I can't believe you said that, Marsha. I practically saved you from getting arrested!"

Marsha stopped. "Oh, forget it."

Collette stood up and frowned down at Marsha.

"So is Sarah coming today or not?" If Sarah wasn't coming, then Collette definitely wouldn't come. But if Sarah was planning on going, Collette had to. She had to try to talk to Sarah.

"Sarah is coming, but she wants you to come, too." Marsha pulled on a leaf and split it up the seam. "My mom said she wouldn't blame you if you didn't show up. Since I *was* a little rude in the car last night."

Collette thought for a moment. If Sarah needed her for moral support, she would show up.

"Are you coming?" asked Marsha. "I'll go if you do. You don't even have to give me another present."

Collette nodded. "Yes, I guess so."

Marsha shot up from the swing and grabbed Collette by the arm. "Great! I promise I won't make you skate with a boy," she added, smiling.

Collette laughed.

"I better go tell my mom the good news," said Marsha as she ran to the side door. "See you this afternoon, Collette."

"Sure," said Collette, waiting for the door to

close. Once it had, she knelt down and pulled the small tissue box from under the tree.

She peered inside.

The china pieces were all still there.

All she had to do now was see if she could fit them together again.

# Chapter Ten

"There, you look as good as new." Collette set Mother Mouse on her dresser and smiled at her. She gave a slight frown at Father Mouse. His nose was definitely not in the tissue box. Even with a dab of brown paint where his nose used to be, he looked different.

"You can use a button for a nose," suggested Laura. "Mommy did that to Buster Bear when Stevie bit his nose off last Christmas."

Collette shook her head. "Father Mouse's head is too little. Maybe the nose is still in Marsha's room. I'll check today."

Laura scrambled on top of the bed and studied Collette. "You look pretty in your new clothes,

Collette. Mommy said you were . . . were starting on stage, or something like that. That's why she got you a new outfit."

Collette picked up the brush and started brushing her ponytail, stretching it till it hung down her back. She knew what Laura was talking about. She'd heard her mother laughing about it on the phone yesterday. "Collette is going to her first boy-girl party, Gail. Can you believe it? Seems like I brought her home from the hospital yesterday and now my little Collette is starting a new stage. . . ."

Plucking two pink tissues from the box, Collette rolled up Mother Mouse carefully. She wouldn't take Father Mouse until she was able to do something with his nose.

"Can't I come?" asked Laura. "I can skate without falling down. I can go two whole times around the rink."

"Next time, Laura. I'd better go now. See you."

Collette stuck the mouse in her pocket as she hurried down the stairs. It was already three-fifteen. She had seen cars pulling up in front of Marsha's house for the last ten minutes.

" 'Bye, I'm leaving!" Collette called as she grabbed her white roller skates by the side door and ran out.

Mother hurried to the top of the steps. "Have fun, honey."

The Cessano's front door swung open before Collette could even put her hand on the heavy brass knocker.

Marsha met her, red-faced and miserable-looking, at the door.

"It's about time!" Marsha huffed as she pulled Collette in by the arm. "I have been waiting for fifteen minutes."

"What's wrong?" Collette dropped her skates on the rug with the others.

Marsha's eyes glistened as she jerked her head toward the large living room. "Listen. . . ."

Collette leaned toward the room. "I don't hear a thing."

"Exactly!" cried Marsha in a miserable voice. "That's the problem. Nobody is talking or laughing. Nobody wants to listen to any tapes." Marsha shoved up her bangs and clenched her teeth. "If only Carole could be here to perk things up."

"Come on," said Collette. She walked into the living room. She certainly didn't want to act like Carole, but she knew how Marsha must be feeling.

As soon as Collette walked into the room, she could feel everyone's discomfort and nervousness. Marsha's living room was like a waiting room at the dentist's office.

The girls were all sitting on the couch, or behind it like some sort of choir. All five of the boys were on the other side of the room, most of them staring out the window as though they wanted to be outside.

"Hi!" said Collette cheerfully. She looked at the fireplace in the center of the room, so she wouldn't have to choose between looking at the girls or the boys.

"Here's Collette," said Marsha, just as cheerfully.

A few girls said a quiet, "Hi." Roger raised his hand in a weak salute. Sarah got up from the couch and hurried over. She was the only one wearing a party dress.

"Collette, look at me," whispered Sarah. She tried to squish down her taffeta skirt. "I don't know

115

what I was thinking about when I got dressed for the party."

Collette glanced down at Sarah's beautiful black patent leather shoes. Sarah was probably thinking about Petey Bennett.

"Run over to my house and borrow a pair of jeans," suggested Collette quickly. "Ask Laura to show you where my red-and-white sweatshirt is."

Sarah reached out and grabbed Collette's hand, giving it a tight squeeze. "Thanks, I was hoping you would say that. I asked Marsha for extra clothes but she just ignored me. I think she's sad 'cause the party is kind of . . . well. . . ."

Sarah giggled. Collette looked around the room, feeling a little sorry for everyone. There was something wrong, but Collette couldn't put her finger on it.

Standing right in the middle of the signpost party, Collette couldn't remember exactly what was so dumb about the idea of a boy-girl party. It wasn't that the boys were invited. In school they didn't bug her that much. Besides, sometimes boys could be really funny in a rude sort of way.

"I wish I could get this tape deck to work!"

announced Marsha with a high laugh. It sounded like she was about to splinter into a thousand pieces.

Collette looked over at the huge tape deck. It had to be Carole's. It was three feet long and had plastic windows and speakers everywhere.

Collette looked over at Roger. Roger probably knew how to work it. Why didn't he just come over and try?

But Roger was busy scratching his neck and pulling at the sleeves of a wool sweater that was so new-looking it was stiff.

Collette took a step closer to John. "Do you know anything about tape decks, John?" Collette asked.

"Yeah, I'll try to fix it." He got up from the window seat and walked over.

For a second, Collette thought Marsha's heart was going to stop. Marsha smiled from ear to ear and then presented the huge tape deck, holding it out toward him like a sacrificial offering.

John put it back on the coffee table and pressed a few buttons. Within seconds, all six girls from the couch were clustered around him. A few of the braver ones, like Meg and Kiersten, were asking questions about the inner workings of the tape deck as though John were the repair man from Sears.

Collette caught Marsha's eye and smiled. At least kids were finally talking.

Marsha pointed to a button and tilted her head. "You are so smart, John!"

The other girls nodded in unison as though they were all observing brain surgery.

Just then the music came on, and everyone clapped.

Collette heard the front door slam and smiled when she saw Sarah. Good, at least she had someone to sit next to now.

"All right, all right, children," cried Mrs. Cessano as she swept briskly into the room.

Collette watched Marsha cringe at the word "children."

"Why don't you turn down that wild-sounding music so we can play a few games before cake and presents. . . ."

"Games?" Marsha yelped. "Mom, no, wait. . . ."

Mrs. Cessano pulled out a small punch-out card and waved it at the crowd. "Now this used to be my absolute favorite. You each punch out a hole, unroll it and read. Maybe you will have to quack like a duck, or walk backwards with your ankle tied to your partner's." Mrs. Cessano laughed at the sheer thought of it all.

A few of the boys were nudging each other. Roger got up and walked out. John McKechnie looked totally bored.

"Mom, wait a second." Marsha rushed over to her mother. Her face was now almost as red as the two iodine circles on her earlobes.

"Punch a hole, punch a hole," encouraged Mrs. Cessano as she walked from Allison to Danielle.

"Isn't this fun?" cried Mrs. Cessano. "And if we hurry, we may have time for one quick game of charades!"

Marsha looked up and glared at Collette from across the room, as if charades had been Collette's idea.

When Mrs. Cessano was standing in front of John, insisting he could hop on one foot and meow if he really wanted to, Collette let herself out the front door. She slid behind the hemlock tree and walked onto the side porch.

She would just wait until everyone was ready to go to the skating rink. She didn't want to go back inside and play silly games and act like she was having fun when she wasn't.

From the living room, Collette could hear the laughter and shouts of the kids who were actually starting to have a great time.

"Can you reach it?"

The voice sounded like Stevie's.

Collette hopped off the swing and peered over the hedge and across the street. Her little brother was standing under the large red maple, pointing and yelling.

"It's way up high, Roger. I think it's in the sky already!"

Collette watched as Roger climbed down from the tree, a large yellow airplane in his hand.

"Boy, are you a good climber!" laughed Stevie as he grabbed the plane from Roger's hand. "Thanks a lot!"

Roger nodded.

"Want me to play with you, Stevie?" asked Roger.

Stevie laughed and shook his head. "No, you are too big."

Roger nodded, shoving both hands inside his pockets. He waved to Stevie and then burst out

120

laughing as Stevie hid behind a hedge and then reappeared by running through the neighbor's flower bed.

Collette stepped behind the hedge as Roger started to cross the street. She didn't want to let Roger know she saw him having more fun outside than inside at the boy-girl party.

As soon as Roger closed the front door, Collette stood up. She better go back in before Marsha realized she was missing. Collette didn't want a fifth grade search party after her. The less attention she got today, the better.

# Chapter Eleven

As Collette got out of the car at Skateland, she looked around. She almost expected fireworks, or at least a small band playing outside the front entrance of the roller rink.

So far Marsha's party had been a little slow. The boys had completely ignored everyone before leaving for the rink. They just gobbled down cake and ice cream and didn't even bother to watch Marsha open her presents.

Collette's fingers closed around the small package in her pocket. She had to find a quieter time to give Marsha her birthday present. She didn't want the boys to hoot and make fun of her for giving such a gift.

Sarah had ridden with Marsha in Mrs. Cessano's car. When she saw Collette, she raced across the parking lot.

"I can't believe we're finally here," Sarah said as she held open the roller rink door for Collette. "And I really can't believe that you decided to come!"

"Me, either," said Collette. She wasn't nervous anymore.

"I think you were right about Petey," said Sarah. "Look at my hair!" She held up a huge clump by her ear. "That idiot stuck his gum in my hair. I can't believe he would do something so . . . so dumb!"

"Maybe it was an accident," offered Collette. She frowned at the huge pink wad of gum in Sarah's beautiful red hair.

Sarah started to giggle.

Collette smiled. "What's so funny?"

"You," laughed Sarah. "You said maybe it was an accident that Petey jabbed his gum in my hair. How could he accidentally do that?"

"Girls, Sarah, Collette . . . look this way!" shouted Mrs. Cessano. She was perched on the railing by the rink door, her leg twisted around the palings like a pipe cleaner. "Wave to me, that's good. All rightee now, hold the doors open wide for the birthday girl. Here she comes . . . here comes Marsha!"

Collette grabbed one side of the door and Sarah swung open the other. They both stepped aside as Marsha walked up the cement ramp.

Marsha waved her arm in the air, swinging it slowly to the left and right as though she were riding on a Rose Bowl float.

Mrs. Cessano leaned closer and closer. "Smile, Marsha!"

Suddenly Marsha reached out and snatched John McKechnie's arm, drawing him closer.

"Oh John, thank you so much for carrying my skates!" she said loudly, winking into the camera.

"Sure," said John shortly. He dropped the skates with a noisy clank and peered out into the crowd.

Marsha shook his arm a little and spoke even more loudly. "Oh John, my mom brought a video camera. This is *so* embarrassing for me. I had no idea she was bringing it to the rink!"

As if on cue, Mrs. Cessano scrambled off the railing and walked toward Marsha and John, using up a quick hundred feet of film. She twisted knobs and yanked out lenses, zooming in and out on every angle of John's cute face.

Collette caught Sarah's eye and they both started to laugh. Marsha had probably begged her mom to get as much of John on film as possible.

"I hope I don't have any trouble getting my skates on," confided Marsha to John. "I'm all thumbs!"

"See you," John answered as he shook free of her and disappeared into the crowd.

Marsha pushed up her bangs with her fist, scowling as she watched him hurry through the doors. Remembering the camera, she turned and waved her mother away.

"Turn it off, Mom. I don't want you to record me being ignored."

"No one can ignore you, Marsha!" laughed Roger as he hurried past. "It's like trying to turn your back on a hurricane!"

Marsha reached over and whacked Roger on the shoulder. "Shut up, Roger! Next time I'll hit you with that ten-ton pig you gave me for my birthday."

Roger and Petey both stuck out their tongues and raced inside.

Collette and Sarah rushed over to Marsha. She looked awful.

"Hurry on inside," said Mrs. Cessano as she snapped on her lens cap. "I want to find a good spot to film."

Marsha nodded glumly. She watched till the doors closed behind her mother before she let out a small shout.

"I can't believe it! Nothing is going right so far!"

Sarah patted Marsha on the back. "Don't worry. When it comes time for the couples' skate, you can ask John and everything will be fine."

Once inside the rink, Collette searched the crowded area for a free bench. She shouted above the P.A. system, "Let's sit over there and put on our skates!"

Now that she was at the rink, she was determined to have a good time.

"I don't even feel like skating now," shouted Marsha as she followed Collette through the crowd. "I can't believe how rude the boys are acting. Don't they realize I paid for them to get in?"

Collette pulled Marsha down on the bench next to her. Sarah squeezed in beside them.

"Just try to have fun, Marsha. You'll be able to skate with John later," said Sarah.

Marsha wasn't paying any attention. Her neck was up as far as it would go, her eyes narrowed to a binocular squint as she peered into the crowd. All of a sudden her eyes popped wide open.

"That creep . . . that . . . that . . . *boy!*" said Marsha between clenched teeth. "Look at that. Just look at that awful John."

Marsha shoved her foot into a skate.

Collette's eyes followed Marsha's extended finger. All three girls stood up and hurried to the railing. John McKechnie was standing close to Susannah, the mysterious seventh-grader. He handed her a glass of soda. She took a sip, then gave it back to John.

"Gross me out!" Marsha spat out each word. "I hope they both catch a terrible case of strep throat."

Sarah laughed. "Look, he bought her a small-size drink. Cheapskate!"

Marsha managed a small smile. "Did you see

that cheapo tape John gave me? I never heard of the group, or any of the songs. I bet he bought it in the dollar bin at the record store."

"Or maybe he got it free in a cereal box!" added Collette.

Marsha snickered. "Look — Susannah is taller than him. If she wants to check out his long eyelashes, she'll have to stoop down."

"Or lift him up on a stool," giggled Sarah.

Collette smiled, glad Marsha was feeling better about things. Looking across the rink at John and Susannah, Collette stopped smiling. John had been so quiet at Marsha's, polite, but not really having a good time. He was laughing now, blowing straw wrappers at Susannah.

Even if Susannah was taller and older than John, she sure made him happy. Something about that made Collette feel better about things. Knowing that John didn't follow the exact rules of the fifth grade made her feel less odd. Everyone liked John, even if he made up his own rules.

"Well, listen guys, I am going to have to go rent my skates before they run out of my size," said Sarah. She patted Marsha on the back again. "I bet John was just nervous about being alone with you, Marsha. That's why he invited Susannah. She's probably a mother figure."

Sarah waved good-bye to both girls as she cut through the crowd.

Marsha's knuckles went white as she gave the railing one final squeeze.

"Well, that does it. My signpost party is an official fizzle, Collette. You were right, as usual. No wonder my mom thinks you are so perfect."

"Oh, I'm not a bit perfect," said Collette quickly. "I make lots of mistakes."

"Name one," said Marsha in a flat voice.

Collette licked her lips and tried to think. She knew she made mistakes, everyone did. But no giant ones jumped out at her.

"See," said Marsha after a second.

"Well . . ." began Collette. "I made a mistake when I said your party would be dumb."

"It is dumb."

"No, I'm having a good time. I mean, this is a really fun party."

Marsha frowned.

"If John wants to hang around Susannah, let him," said Collette brightly. "I think you're a lot cuter."

Both girls watched the skaters zooming past. Roger reached out and tried to grab a handful of Marsha's hair.

"Seaweed — Seaweed!" he cried.

Marsha jumped back from the railing. "Go break your neck, Roger!" she yelled after him.

As Marsha clomped back to the bench with her one skate on, she sighed, "It's my own fault. I expected too much from this party. I thought I would turn into a different person, or know how to act with boys. I thought I would be more like Susannah Thacker."

"I know how you feel, Marsha. I felt the same way after the first day of kindergarten. I thought I would know how to read, like magic, after one day, and I didn't."

Marsha slid her other foot into a skate and pounded it up and down on the wooden floor. "And the way I listened to Carole. Boy . . . I haven't even told my dad about the mouse family. He'll never want to buy me anything else again."

Digging deep into her pocket, Collette drew out the tiny package.

"Happy birthday, Marsha!"

Marsha took the present and looked up at Collette.

"But I said you didn't have to give me another present. You already gave me the money at the mall."

Collette laughed and shook her head. "That was Carole's idea for a birthday present. This present is *my* idea."

"Thanks," said Marsha as she unrolled the package.

A small white china mouse rolled out onto Marsha's palm. The tiny white apron had been glued so carefully only a thin line remained on the smooth china surface.

"Mother Mouse," said Marsha softly.

Collette pointed to the tail.

"I found all three parts, so it still curls up."

Marsha's hand shook a little as she took a deep breath.

"My dad carried the mouse family home in a box all the way from Chicago," began Marsha tearfully. "He was afraid the baggage guys might throw his suitcase and. . . ."

Collette watched as Marsha gently rewrapped

Mother Mouse and pushed her deep into her tennis shoe.

"Thanks a lot, Collette. I'll put her back on my shelf as soon as I get home."

"And I'm going to glue the rest of the mice tomorrow," promised Collette. "We just have to find Father Mouse's nose."

Marsha stood up, smiling. "Hey, maybe I could help you. After the party, I mean."

"Sure. I have all the pieces in a box under my bed."

Collette pushed her feet into the skates and pulled the laces tight.

"I'm almost ready."

The announcer at the rink was asking for all skaters to please clear the floor when Sarah skated up to them.

"Petey asked me if I wanted to skate," Sarah laughed. She slid onto the bench beside Collette. "Can you believe it?" Sarah made a face. "I told him to go chew some more gum and stick himself to the wall."

Collette laughed the loudest. Marsha shrugged and sighed at the same time.

"Well, I hope someone gets to skate with a boy

for the couples' skate. My mom hasn't filmed anything since we've been inside."

"The next skate will be a ladies' choice. . . . The next skate . . ."

Marsha began to smile before the announcer had even finished.

"Hey, great idea! I won't have to wait for John to ask me. I'll ask him."

"Marsha, I thought you didn't like John anymore," Collette said. She stood up and clomped over to the railing.

"I don't," laughed Marsha as she hurried onto the floor. "But he sure will look great on film."

Sarah and Collette held onto each other as Marsha shot across the floor to where John stood with Petey.

"Oh, no," whispered Collette. She saw Susannah get to John first, grabbing his arm and pulling him out onto the floor.

"Poor Marsha," said Sarah.

Collette felt someone pulling her ponytail. She twisted around and saw Roger, grinning.

"Want to skate, Collette?"

Somehow Roger had missed the fact that it was a ladies' choice. Collette wasn't surprised.

Collette looked at Sarah, then over at Marsha, who was heading toward them with a pout pulling down her whole face.

"Roger, ask Marsha to skate, okay?" Collette talked quickly, trying to convince Roger before Marsha got to them.

Roger didn't try to hide his disappointment.

"Why? I asked *you*."

Collette glanced over her shoulder, then took a step closer to Roger.

"I . . . I was going to ask you for the all-couples' skate, Roger, so . . ."

"You were?" asked Sarah.

"You were?" repeated Roger.

Collette shrugged her shoulders, trying not to smile. "Yeah. Why not? To thank you for getting Stevie's plane out of the tree and everything."

Roger's face got a little red. He nodded his head like he thought the plan sounded pretty good.

"So ask Marsha now, and then I'll . . . I'll find you later."

Collette gave Roger a push in Marsha's direction.

Sarah nodded her head. "Yeah, to thank Marsha for the party."

Marsha stormed across the floor.

"Boy, oh boy!" she fumed. "Did you see that?"

"Want to skate, Marsha?" Roger's voice squeaked when he got to the word "skate."

Marsha looked up, frowning . . . waiting. "Is this some sort of joke, Roger?"

Roger smiled, holding out both hands to show his innocence.

Marsha looked at each hand, then over her shoulder at her mother, who was perched on a bench near the snack bar, camera hoisted up on her shoulder.

"Oh . . . oh, all right," said Marsha at last. She reached out and grabbed Roger by the hand. "I guess you'll have to do, Roger. Just remember, when we skate past my mom, be sure and look like you're having fun!"

Roger twisted his head and crossed his eyes at Sarah and Collette.

The girls watched as Marsha raced slightly ahead of Roger, yanking him up beside her, then dragging him behind by his arm.

"That was nice of Roger," said Sarah at last. "I didn't think he'd do it."

Collette nodded. She thought so, too.

Sarah nudged Collette. "Remember you have to skate with him later. You promised."

"I know. It won't be too bad, I guess."

"Yeah," agreed Sarah. "I guess if you ask Roger, I'll ask Petey. Just so I won't be all alone. I'll make him spit his gum out first."

Collette looked at Sarah and smiled.

"Want to skate, Sarah?"

Sarah looked out at the floor. "Collette, we can't. I think it's a boy-girl kind of thing."

Collette laughed and skated out onto the wooden floor.

"It is not. The announcer said ladies' choice. That's the only rule he gave."

Sarah scratched her head, giggling as her fingers got caught in the wad of gum.

"You're right. Come on, Collette."

As Collette grabbed onto Sarah's hand, she gave it a nice, tight squeeze. The air rushing through her hair felt great. She looked over at Sarah, and then down at the bits of dancing light sparkling on the floor.

"Now remember what Marsha said, Sarah. When we go past Mrs. Cessano and her camera, be sure to smile and wave and act like you're having a lot of fun!"

"Yes, sir!" laughed Sarah. Collette began to skate faster than ever, pulling Sarah around the bend with a whiplike swing.

Collette sped past John and Susannah, Lorraine and Petey, and finally Marsha and Roger.

By the time she flew past Mrs. Cessano, Collette forgot to fling out her hand and wave. She was having too much fun!